THE GAMBLER GRIMOIRE

BR KINGSOLVER

The Gambler Grimoire

By BR Kingsolver

brkingsolver.com

Cover art by Heather Hamilton-Senter
www.bookcoverartistry.com

Copyright 2021 BR Kingsolver

License Notes

This book is licensed for your personal enjoyment only. All rights reserved. No part of this book may be reproduced or transmitted in any form or by any means now known or hereinafter invented, electronic or mechanical, including but not limited to photocopying, recording, or by an information storage and retrieval system, without the written permission of the Publisher, except where permitted by law.

In ebook or other electronic format, it may not be re-sold or given away to other people. If you would like to share this book with another person, please purchase an additional copy for each recipient. If you're reading this book and did not purchase it, or it was not purchased for your use only, then please return it and purchase your own copy. Thank you for respecting the hard work of this author.

❦ Created with Vellum

BOOKS BY BR KINGSOLVER

Wicklow College of Arcane Arts

The Gambler Grimoire

The Revenge Game

The Rift Chronicles

Magitek

War Song

Soul Harvest

Rosie O'Grady's Paranormal Bar and Grill

Shadow Hunter

Night Stalker

Dark Dancer

Well of Magic

Knights Magica

The Dark Streets Series

Gods and Demons

Dragon's Egg

Witches' Brew

The Chameleon Assassin Series

Chameleon Assassin

Chameleon Uncovered

Chameleon's Challenge

Chameleon's Death Dance

Diamonds and Blood

The Telepathic Clans Saga
The Succubus Gift
Succubus Unleashed
Broken Dolls
Succubus Rising
Succubus Ascendant

Other books
I'll Sing for my Dinner
Trust

Short Stories in Anthologies
Here, Kitty Kitty
Bellator

~~~

CHAPTER 1

A movement to my left caught my eye. Above me, a man standing in a second-story corner window was looking down on my mini-circus. He was middle-aged, with dark hair and a beard, and wearing a tweed jacket. He didn't smile or frown. He could have been the poster boy for an Oxford don. I chuckled to myself, wondering what the uniform for female faculty entailed.

I paid the taxi driver and crawled out onto the sidewalk. A four-hour plane ride to Pittsburgh, followed by the hour-long taxi ride to Wicklow, had left me stiff. The driver pulled my bags from the trunk and set them down. I gripped my purse and computer bag. At that point, two porters emerged from the building.

"Dr. Robinson?" one asked.

"Yes, I'm Dr. Robinson."

"This way, ma'am. The stuff you shipped ahead arrived yesterday."

I looked up, and up, at the three-story Gothic Revival building in front of me. I had dreamed about working on that campus, teaching there, and my dream had come through.

I followed the porters up the broad front steps with a metal railing in the middle, then through a high, pointed archway. A long, wide, paved breezeway open to the sky ended at another arched opening. Doors were regularly spaced off the open arcade on both sides. There weren't any windows on any level.

To my surprise, the porters immediately turned right through the first of two doorways next to each other. A small brass plaque—shiny and new—on the open door read, 'Savanna Robinson, PhD.'

A short hallway with a table on one side and a wardrobe on the other led to a fairly spacious room—as large as my whole apartment in Oakland. It was furnished with heavy wood-and-leather couches and chairs, and two heavy coffee tables. One wall was covered with empty built-in bookshelves that ended at a window overlooking the street where the taxi had let me off. In front of the built-in bookshelves sat the boxes I had shipped from the West Coast. My books, tools, clothing, and the rest of my few personal effects.

Next to the window, a massive stone fireplace covered half of that wall. The other walls were covered in deep red wallpaper above walnut wainscoting. All of the trim around the doors and windows, the crown molding, and the baseboard were a deep, rich walnut color.

The room would have been very dark, except the wall opposite the entrance hallway was almost all glass, with a view to the outside. That was south, I realized. I could plant herbs and flowers along the windows.

Along the wall to my left, there were three doors. The porters came out of the middle one, handed me a set of keys, bade me good day, and left. I wandered over to the room they had come out of and found a bedroom with an attached bathroom. The claw-foot tub looked inviting, but my first thought was whether there would be enough hot water to fill it. In Oakland, I had learned to shower very quickly.

The doorway next to the outside door revealed the kitchen. Not the fanciest or the largest kitchen I'd ever cooked in, or the most modern, but if the appliances all worked, I decided it would do. There was only one window, looking out over the back porch and stairs down to the garden.

The kitchen was stocked with everything except food. The cabinets were filled with dishes, pots and pans, and tableware. Everything looked rather old but in good shape, from the floral-designed china and formal tea service to the cast-iron pans and the Dutch oven.

I walked to the wall of windows and gazed out into an herb and flower garden contained within a space between a wall on the street and the building that extended beyond my apartment. The door between the windows and the kitchen opened to a stairway leading down into the garden. The narrow path through the garden led to a greenhouse. That brought a smile to my face, and I immediately opened the door, walked down the wooden stairs, and wandered among the plants.

Looking back to my apartment, I saw windows on the two floors above mine, and I wondered who lived above me.

I felt like dancing, but I didn't know who might be watching. Perhaps more dour professors, like the one who watched me arrive.

A nice salary, with a free place to live included, was more than I could have hoped for at any of Wicklow's rival institutions. On the whole, quite satisfactory. And Wicklow College of the Arcane Arts was the oldest, most prestigious institution of arcane study in North America. In fact, other than two colleges in the United Kingdom and one in France, there wasn't a school remotely resembling Wicklow.

I decided I didn't care who might be watching and danced down the pathway, singing to myself. I had hit the jackpot!

CHAPTER 2

The whole apartment had a heavy, dark, masculine vibe. I placed the few knickknacks, pictures, and other things I had brought to try and provide a little color and femininity to the place. But when I finished with that, I looked around and realized I would need more to enliven the place.

The man overlooking the sitting area from the large, nineteenth-century portrait above the fireplace would probably have to stay. I assumed someone would have a fit if I took him down. And where would I hide it? It was too large to hang in the guest washroom.

I put my clothes away. There was plenty of storage in the apartment. A nice pantry in the kitchen, a large walk-in closet and a wardrobe in the bedroom, a linen closet in the bathroom, and a wardrobe that doubled as a coat closet in the entry hall. In addition to a walk-in closet and a wardrobe, the bedroom also had a chest of drawers.

I had started on the boxes of books when there was a knock at the door. I opened it and found myself looking at a tall, willowy blonde woman wearing wire-rim glasses. She was maybe ten years younger than I was. Her white blouse under a short black jacket and a black skirt that hit the top of her knees was basically the kind of outfit that I usually wore when lecturing.

"Dr. Robinson? I'm Kelly Grace, the college librarian." I thought I detected a hint of a British accent.

"Hi, come in," I said. "The place is a bit of a mess. I haven't finished unpacking yet."

Kelly smiled. "It always takes me weeks to find everything when I move, and you've barely arrived. I thought I'd drop by and welcome you to Wicklow. Has Dr. Carver stopped in?"

Carver was the dean who hired me. "No, other than the porters, you're the first person I've met. Would you like some tea? I think I know where to find it, and there's a kettle in the kitchen."

Kelly sat at the small kitchen table while I bustled around, rinsing the kettle and putting it on to boil.

"I feel a little like I'm in a museum," I said. "Or in my grandmother's kitchen."

Kelly laughed. "It's part of Wicklow's charm. Give it thirty or forty years, and you'll hardly notice it. I had a feeling Carver hadn't showed up. He's not known for his social graces."

"I have an appointment with him in the morning. I've met him only once," I said, "and spoken with him on the phone a couple of times. He flew out to San Francisco to interview me."

The kettle whistled, and I poured hot water in the teapot, then brought it and two teacups to the table.

"I'm afraid I don't have any cookies or anything," I said. "You know, I was rather taken by surprise that Dr. Carver flew out. Maybe he just wanted an excuse to go to San Francisco, but in my experience, candidates are always brought in for interviews."

Kelly's eyebrows raised slightly at that news. "Have you ever been to Wicklow before?" she asked.

"Oh, yes. Once about seven years ago, and again three years ago. I presented a couple of papers at conferences here. I fell in love with the place. I met Dr. Carver then, but when he interviewed me, he didn't act like he remembered me."

Kelly appeared to be suppressing a grin. "As I said, he's not really a people person. The stereotypical absent-minded professor. He's much more comfortable in a laboratory, with his head buried in arcane formulae and incantations. There's an old rumor that he was promoted to dean because he was so bad in the classroom. But, yes, usually candidates are brought in. Your recruitment was a bit unusual."

"That's what I thought. Wicklow did advertise a couple of positions for this fall, but they were posted in March of *last* year. They were in areas other than mine, though. Then, when the college advertised for this position in April of *this* year—to start this fall—I thought it strange, rather hurried."

I poured the tea while Kelly sort of cocked her head to one side and asked, "Out of curiosity, what did Carver say about why the position was open?"

"I asked, of course, and he said the incumbent had left suddenly and without notice. It put the administration in a bit of a bind, I guess, having to fill the position as an emergency." I grinned. "I was able to negotiate it as tenure-track. He seemed rather desperate."

Kelly laughed. "Oh, that is rich. Accurate, I guess. Yes, Dr. Kavanaugh did leave his post rather abruptly, and he didn't give any notice. He was murdered."

"Here?" I glanced toward the doorway to the sitting room.

"Oh, no. This wasn't his place, but yes, in his apartment in this building. Bludgeoned to death with a fireplace poker. A very stereotypical way to die, don't you think? I thought it was in keeping with the traditional, stodgy Wicklow atmosphere. Agatha Christie would have approved."

"Did they catch who did it?"

Kelly shook her head. "Not a clue. Of course, everyone on campus has their own pet theory and suspects."

"Who investigates crimes here?" I asked.

"The campus police, who are all witches, and the city cops, who are generally not. Mostly, the city stays away from here, but there is one detective, Lieutenant Sam Kagan, who is a witch and assigned to the campus, and the city chief of police is a witch, as is the mayor. Kagan doesn't have much to do, since there's almost no serious crime here. You are aware of the situation with the city, aren't you?"

"I know that a lot of witches live here," I said.

"Yes. It's estimated that between a quarter and a third of the population are witches, and maybe another fifth have other paranormal abilities or are not human, if you know what I mean. In my experience, the majority of the city believes in paranormal abilities, and those who don't must be willfully ignorant. We don't flaunt it, but no one takes particular care to hide it, either."

"You don't have a vampire problem, do you? Parts of San Francisco are practically overrun with them."

"No, but there are a few wolf shifters here. Lots of forests and mountains in the area. They usually keep to themselves. Unless you're into that sort of thing, stay away from a biker bar called the Wolf's Den."

Kelly invited me to dinner that evening. "I have a car, I can show you some of the city, and we can swing by a grocery store on the way home."

"That would be great. Thank you." As I showed Kelly out, I said, "Oh, there was a man watching me from that window over there when I arrived."

"Dark hair, beard, maybe a bit of salt-and-pepper? Dr. Hamilton. David Hamilton. Elemental magic. Rather a traditionalist, been here a long time. I'm not sure he's completely comfortable with all the new women faculty, but he's civil. He was a friend of Brett's." I must have looked a bit puzzled because Kelly clarified. "Dr. Brett Kavanaugh, the man who was murdered."

CHAPTER 3

Kelly was a Wicklow graduate who had gone on to take a master's degree in library science at the University of Maryland before returning to Wicklow as the library's associate director. She took the top job when her boss retired.

She gave me a whirlwind tour of the city. As she drove me around, she told me about the city and the college. Some of it I already knew, but it was interesting to hear about it from one who obviously fancied herself as an area historian.

"This is all here because of John Howard, bastard son of the fourth Earl of Wicklow. His father packed him off to the New World because not only was he a witch—inherited from his mother—but also a bit of a rake who caused his father some embarrassment," Kelly said with a grin. "The earl evidently also supplied him with enough money to start a very successful business in Philadelphia. But there was some sort of scandal involving the daughter of a wealthy merchant, the daughter of a preacher, and a woman who told fortunes. As far as I can determine, they all became pregnant at about the same time, which angered not only their families but also the young ladies themselves."

Kelly took a turn that led us away from downtown. "I come up here to be alone sometimes," she said as two more turns put us on a winding road up a steep hill. When we reached the top, the road ended in a small parking lot.

"There are hiking trails from here," Kelly said, unbuckling her seat belt and getting out of the car.

I followed her. We walked about fifty feet along the trail in front of the car, and it opened up into a glade at the top of the low mountain. Wicklow was below us. It looked like a normal, sleepy rural town with a river running through it, but the massive stone buildings of the college on the south edge of the city reminded me of a castle looming over a village in the English countryside.

"As I was saying," Kelly resumed, "John Howard left Philadelphia rather in a hurry, selling his business, and evidently taking some of his clients' money as well. He came out here, bought land, and built the college. The first building is that one, Howard Hall, his home."

She took a deep breath, then wandered over to a large fallen log and sat down. "I don't know if he had the idea of the college at first, or it came to him later. The workmen and their families were the first settlers in the area. And since construction continued for almost eighty years, the town sort of grew around them."

"It's beautiful here," I said, sitting down beside her. "So green and peaceful. I see why you like it."

"I've traveled a bit, spent a year bumming about Europe, and another year working in a bookstore in London, but I haven't found anywhere I'd rather live. It is a bit sparse as far as nightlife, and there is a dearth of eligible bachelors, but anytime I get lonely for city life, I can drive into Pittsburgh for the weekend."

Kelly then took me to a charming bistro overlooking the river where we had dinner and a couple of glasses of wine.

Afterward, we went to a grocery store that looked like any other modern American grocery on the outside, but most of the produce and meat was organic and locally-sourced.

"Not all the witches live in town," Kelly said. "A lot of the farms around here are owned by the descendants of the original settlers, who were all witches. The other farmers tend to follow the same practices, as that's what people buy."

When I got back to my apartment, I opened the front door and felt around for a light switch. Not finding one, I fished in my purse and found the small flashlight I always carried. Looking around the foyer, I still couldn't find a switch, but then I shone the light on the ceiling, and realized why. There was a magelight attached to the ceiling, but no electric light as far as I could see.

I spoke a Word, and the light came on. I continued into the sitting room, and the flashlight revealed several more magelights attached to the walls. The situation was the same in the kitchen, bedroom, and the bathroom.

The stove and oven were gas. Then I discovered the refrigerator was plugged in, as was the clothes washer. Each had a single socket connected to conduit attached to the wall. With no automatic dishwasher, obviously I would be doing my dishes in the sink with its drainboard next to it. The full import of living in a hundred-and-fifty-year-old building crashed down on me, and I had to laugh.

There wasn't any electricity in the bathroom or bedroom, so I might as well not have packed my blow dryer. Then I panicked as I wondered how I was supposed to charge my phone and computer. Unplug the fridge?

Some frantic searching led to the discovery of four sockets and a wi-fi router hidden away under the desk in the sitting room. I plugged in my laptop and phone, and my near-hysteria dissolved when the computer asked me for a password to connect to the college wi-fi network. I half expected the landline phone on the desk to have a rotary dial, but it was pushbutton.

As I made myself an omelet and cut up some fresh fruit, I mused about my evening with Kelly. It turned out the young woman was somewhat more than the 'college librarian.' Her official title was Archivist and Director of Library Services, with employees in the library, plus student aides, and more full-time employees in the small college museum. She evidently also managed the bookstore and academic computer services. Impressive for a thirty-one-year-old woman in a staid environment such as Wicklow College.

Sitting with my tea after breakfast, I suddenly realized I'd been woolgathering and had only an hour before my appointment with Dr. Carver. I jumped up from my chair at the kitchen table, quickly washed the breakfast dishes, took a quick shower, and pulled a business suit from the closet.

I hurried out, locked the door, and walked through the breezeway between the two halves of the building. On each side, there were ten sets of two doors. Emerging from under the arch at the far end, I stood admiring the wide, open expanse of lawn surrounded by stately three- and four-story buildings that was Howard Quadrangle.

Glancing at the map Kelly had given me, I noted the names of the buildings. John Howard had been an Oxford man, and he envisioned his college in light of what he was familiar with. Of course, what I was looking at was originally the entire college, but it had grown since.

Across from me, about fifty yards away, was another arch like the one I stood under. I followed a sidewalk through the green space, through the arch, and into the next quadrangle, and then to the Administration Building.

Dr. Jerome Carver was a small, thin man in his fifties with a potbelly. Wire-rimmed glasses sat on a slightly bulbous nose, and his shiny bald head was ringed with light brown hair. He wore the same herringbone-tweed jacket with leather patches at the elbows as when I met him in San Francisco.

He stood when I came into his office but didn't extend his hand. I wondered if it was because he was old-fashioned or because we were witches. Many witches avoided touching other people.

"Dr. Robinson, so good of you to come. Please, sit down. I trust that your accommodations are satisfactory?"

"Oh, yes. Thank you."

"Well, I have a few things to go over with you, and then I'll give you a tour, if that's all right."

He handed me a stack of papers, with a map and a small blue booklet, the cover of which said, "Wicklow College, Faculty Handbook." I opened it and saw that it was handwritten in an archaic cursive script, and had been photocopied, then stapled together.

"If you have any questions after you've read it, please ask me," he said. "I'll just hit a couple of specific things. It's probably not necessary, but I think it's important to emphasize that intimate relations with students are completely prohibited, and it's a terminating event. That doesn't mean you can't have a beer with a student who is of age, or have a promising student or students to your apartment for a meal, but please, maintain a professional relationship."

I smiled and swallowed my reaction. "I'm not attracted to men twenty years younger than I am, Dr. Carver, but I understand the need to emphasize the point."

He nodded and seemed to relax a little. "Also, although relations between faculty, and with staff, are not prohibited, we do ask that while on campus, and in public, we expect discretion and a professional demeanor, especially anywhere students might be present."

I nodded, maintaining my smile. "Yes, I understand the need to provide students with proper role models. And you're not going to see me dancing at a disco in a skirt that doesn't cover my backside. I do have experience with students and their fantasies, and I prefer to prevent uncomfortable situations."

To my surprise, that actually got a chuckle from him. I hadn't guessed that he had a sense of humor.

"Now, with the unpleasant things aside, you'll find your class schedule in there," he motioned at the stack of papers. "Normally, you would be assigned two classes, with labs and tutorials, because of your duties with the herb garden and the greenhouse. But I'm afraid that we're a bit short staffed this term. You'll have to take a third class, but we will pay you extra."

"Greenhouse and herb garden? You mean those outside my door?"

"Yes. That's why we gave you that apartment. You don't have to tend it all yourself, of course. There are two graduate students and three student aides who do most of the work, but you will have to supervise them."

"I see. I don't remember seeing anything about that in my contract."

Carver looked distinctly uncomfortable.

"And why are you short staffed?" I asked, wondering if he would tell me about Kavanaugh's murder.

"Mrs. Donnelly, the greenhouse manager, resigned at the end of the spring term. We are recruiting for the position, but at the earliest, we might manage to find someone to start in January."

He cleared his throat and adjusted his tie. "As to the faculty shortage, I'm afraid that is my fault. You have an unusual skill set, as did your predecessor. Until he left, we didn't understand just how unusual. I've also applied to add two more faculty positions, one in Alchemy and another in Apothecary Arts. I'm afraid we've discovered a problem with having all our eggs in one basket, so to speak."

"And why did my predecessor leave?" I asked, half holding my breath waiting for an answer.

"I'm sorry to say that he died suddenly. It wasn't anything anyone expected."

I leaned forward. "Dr. Carver, I know how Dr. Kavanaugh died. Am I safe here? Is this campus safe?"

He bit his lip and sat back in his chair, steepling his fingertips. "I wish I could say yes, Dr. Robinson. I think so, but since we don't know who killed Dr. Kavanaugh, or why, I would be lying if I tried to give you some kind of certainty. I can say that there hasn't been a faculty murder in the past twenty years. As I'm sure you know, there is some element of danger at any institution such as Wicklow. Young, emotional people with untrained, powerful magic are our occupational hazard."

Nodding, I said, "Yes, that I quite understand. There were a couple of incidents where I was teaching in San Francisco. Thank you for being honest with me." I did notice the caveats in what he said. No *faculty* murders. That, of course, raised the question of staff and student murders. And what about the faculty member killed twenty years before?

"However," I continued, "I'm afraid that taking a full class load as well as a second full-time job running your horticultural operation is out of the question. As I said, it's not in my contract, and I wouldn't have agreed to such an arrangement if you had presented it to me. I can, however, provide a suitable candidate. A recently granted doctorate who studied under me in Sausalito. His name's Steven McCallum. I'll have him contact you. Dr. Carver, do we understand each other?"

Carver hesitated, then nodded. "Can I at least count on you

to supervise the greenhouse staff until we get someone in? I wouldn't know where to begin."

I took pity on him. "Yes, but just until you hire someone. Soon."

Carver gave me a weak smile. "Thank you. And now, shall we go explore your new home?"

CHAPTER 4

Carver led me down the hall from his office. We passed through an arch. On one side, a plaque said *Department of Alchemy*. A plaque on the other wall read *Department of Healing and Apothecary Arts*. At the end, he showed me a small office overlooking what my map identified as Scholars' Quad.

"This is your office. This building is almost deserted at night, but it's close to the classrooms, and you can meet students here during the day. For your tutorials, you can hold them either in your apartment, in any unused classroom—just book it with my secretary—or in one of the available rooms in the library."

He handed me an old-fashioned key, and I opened the door. The office was clean, no dust, but there were books on the shelves and a stack of papers on the desk. I checked the desk and found pens, paperclips, and other office supplies. There were files in the bottom left drawer. The bottom right drawer didn't open, but I didn't detect any magic. It was just locked, and there wasn't a key around that I could see.

Carver went over and pulled open the top drawer of a filing cabinet.

"I thought someone had cleaned out this office. I'm so sorry. I'll send someone immediately."

I shrugged. "Perhaps Dr. Kavanaugh's family might like some of the things." Walking over to the bookshelf, I scanned the titles. "But anything they don't want, such as these books probably, can stay."

"He didn't have any family," Carver said.

"Oh. Well, if I could just get some boxes, I can sort through all this and box up what I don't find useful. No sense in having people take the paperclips when I would just have to order more, and some of these books would interest no one but another practitioner."

Carver stood, wringing his hands and looking around. "Yes, yes, of course. I'm so sorry." As he walked out into the hall, I could hear him mumbling, "I was sure I told someone to clean that office. It was such a distressing time."

Glancing out the window, I noticed that the office was at the northeast corner of the Quad. Past the arch in the building on the south would be Howard Quad and my apartment. It was a bit of a hike, but nothing like Sausalito where the Institute's buildings were scattered all over town.

I took another look at the locked drawer, then followed Carver out, locking the office door and dropping the key in my purse.

Tracing our steps back down the hall to the stairway, we went down to the ground floor, and then through an outside door at the back of the building. Carver stopped at the bottom. In front of us stood the large Classical Greek building that I recognized as the library from my previous visits. Possibly the largest arcane library in North America, although it held far more books than just those dealing with magic and other arcane subjects.

"John Howard Library," Carver said. "And there, the Howard Museum of Arcane Arts." He motioned with his left hand toward a set of steps leading to another doorway. They exactly matched the steps and the doorway into the library on my right.

Carver took me into the library and introduced me to Kelly. As he did so, we exchanged glances, and she winked at me. She had a sparkle in her eye and a slight grin. Neither of us mentioned that we had met before.

Next, he took me around and showed me the classroom buildings, including the three rooms where I would be teaching that term. From there, we trekked over to John Howard's original mansion. That was where the college president lived and entertained, and the building also held the conference center and a theater.

He pointed out a building containing laboratories for physical sciences and magic, and the campus recreational center past the Howard House, but thankfully, didn't make me trek over there.

The last places Carver wanted to show me were my laboratory, the herb garden, and the greenhouse. I was wearing flats, and by the time we had marched all the way back to his office, I was glad of that.

The labs were in a two-story concrete building between my apartment and the greenhouse. There was an outside door to the building facing the student dormitories, and one opened from the herb garden directly into my lab.

"All the biological labs are in this building," Carver said. "Medical labs are upstairs. Labs for physical and elemental magic are in the building north of the museum. As you can imagine, it is heavily warded. We wouldn't want any accidents getting out of hand."

I fought to hide a smile. He said it so matter-of-factly, as though students and untrained magicians throughout history hadn't left steaming craters, massive forest fires, and demolished buildings as testaments to their mistakes.

When we reached the herb garden, Dr. Carver said, "Dr. Kavanaugh supervised the greenhouse staff, including the students.

The laboratory and the workshop were about what I expected as far as equipment and tools. The first room next to the herb garden looked like a normal gardener's workshop. Pots, bins with potting soil, other planting media, fertilizer, and wooden workbenches.

In one of the rooms, we discovered a woman busy packing things into a box. We evidently startled her, and she whirled around.

I judged her to be in her fifties, her past-shoulder-length dark hair liberally sprinkled with gray. She had piercing blue eyes and a hawk's beak nose jutted over thin lips. Her clothes were sixties counterculture—a blue shirt with bloused sleeves, multiple necklaces and earrings, and a brown ankle-length skirt of a soft fabric, possibly velvet.

"Oh, you startled me," she said. "I was just clearing some of my personal things."

"Agnes," Carver said, "This is Dr. Robinson, the new apothecary professor." He turned toward me. "Agnes Bishop also teaches some of our Apothecary Arts courses. She's part-time."

I stepped forward and held out my hand. "Call me Savanna. I'm pleased to meet you."

Agnes shot a glance at the offered hand and took a step back, tucking her own hands behind her back. "Welcome aboard. I was just clearing my stuff out."

"That's all right," I said, looking around. "You don't have to. I'm sure there's plenty of room for both of us."

Agnes fidgeted, her gaze darting around the room. "No, I have my own place. I like things a certain way. I'll be out of here today."

"Are any of the girls about today?" Carver asked.

Agnes turned away to continue boxing her tools. "Emma's in the greenhouse."

Since he obviously felt the conversation was at an end, Carver moved on to the next room, and I followed him. That room was an alchemist's lab with white walls, floor and ceiling, stainless steel workbenches, and far more sophisticated equipment.

"Agnes is a bit eccentric," Carver said, "and I guess I should warn you that she wasn't happy that we hired you instead of promoting her. But she's basically an herbalist, and her only academic credentials are a bachelor's degree in English. She owns an apothecary shop in town, selling herbs and touristy witchcraft items. She worked part-time here in the greenhouse and taught a class each trimester. Two classes this trimester."

"Was the apartment hers?" I asked.

"Oh, no. She lives in town. That apartment has been empty for the past twelve years."

We passed back through the rooms to the herb garden and walked down the path to the greenhouse. It turned out to be far larger than I expected, and was divided inside into three different climate zones. The laboratory building and the faculty apartments shielded its north side.

"Is the greenhouse manager expected to maintain the facility itself?" I asked out of curiosity. "All the heaters, the water system, the air conditioning?" I knew the programming alone was a major task. Seeing the size of the place, I was even more convinced that I was smart to put my foot down and not take on the additional work. The greenhouse was commercial size, as large as the student dormitory buildings.

Carver answered, "Oh, no. Of course not. We have a contract with a company in Pittsburgh. They have a full-time maintenance engineer stationed here in Wicklow. You can get a copy of the contract from my secretary, if you wish."

In the second section, we found a slender young woman with brown hair pulled into a ponytail, tending to the plants.

"Emma!" Carver called. "Come here, please."

The woman put down whatever she was doing, pulled off her gloves, and strolled over. She wore a white t-shirt and jeans.

"Emma, this is Dr. Robinson, the new apothecary professor."

The young woman smiled and offered her hand, which I took, in spite of the dirt. "So glad to meet you. Emma Hall. I guess you're my new dissertation professor?" Her eyes shifted to Carver briefly, then back.

"I don't know," I said. "What are you studying?"

"I started my doctoral program in Apothecary Arts last fall, but things got kind of interrupted in the spring. Can we talk about it?"

The earnest, pleading look on her face tugged at my heart. "Of course, we can. Were you studying under Dr. Kavanaugh?"

Emma nodded.

I turned to Carver. "Do I need to be anywhere tomorrow morning?"

He shook his head. "I had meant to speak to you about Dr. Kavanaugh's graduate students."

"Just send them along, and we'll work it out. Emma, are you free at eight in the morning?"

"Yes, ma'am," she said enthusiastically.

I pointed in the direction of my apartment. "Breakfast. Eight o'clock sharp. Bring what you have."

"Yes, ma'am!"

As we were speaking, a gray tabby cat strolled by.

"Another student, or just one of the greenhouse staff?" I asked.

Emma laughed. "Koshka is our rodent control expert. Her buddy Pete stays outside and patrols the garden. I've been feeding them over the summer, but Lia is the one who mostly takes care of them."

I strolled with Carver back to the Administration Building, and he took his leave. I went to my new office, locked the door behind me, and sat in the chair behind the desk. With a quick spell, it took no time to unlock the desk drawer. Pulling it open, I found a dozen file folders.

Knocking on the door drew my attention. I shoved the files back in the drawer, closed it, and went to the door. When I opened it, a tall, handsome, dark-haired man in the evidently *de rigueuer* tweed jacket stood there.

"Dr. Robinson?"

"Yes?"

He smiled—a very pleasant smile. "I'm Anton Ricard, chairman of the Alchemy Department. I saw you come in and wanted to catch you and welcome you."

I returned the smile. "Thank you. I just found my office, and it seems still to be full of Dr. Kavanaugh's stuff."

He craned his neck and looked over my shoulder, then sighed. "So it seems. Speak with Katy. I won't keep you, but there is a faculty meeting on Monday. Twelve o'clock in the faculty dining room."

"Okay. Thank you."

"And did Jerome tell you about the reception Monday evening?"

"He mentioned it."

He gave a bit of a snort and a chuckle. "President's ballroom. Did he show you where that is?"

"Oh, yes, I know where it is."

"Seven o'clock for cocktails. It's a formal tradition Dr. Phillips takes very seriously. He thinks we should all be friendly and socialize with each other."

I smiled. "Thank you for warning me."

He nodded. "I'll see you Monday." He turned to walk away.

"Oh, Dr. Ricard!" I called, and the man turned back to me. "Who is the chairman of Apothecary Arts?"

He shrugged. "I don't know. Dr. Kavanaugh was." He flashed a mischievous grin. "Maybe you are."

I watched him walk away and enter the room three doors down across the hall. He moved like an athlete and was worth watching.

Closing the door, I locked it again and went back to the desk. I picked up the first file, labeled "GG," and opened it. It looked to be personal correspondence, but the name of the sender caught my attention. Harold Merriweather had a rare bookstore in London. I had been there several times, since he not only sold normal rare books but was also probably the most well-known dealer in arcane texts in the English-speaking world. He also brokered arcane artifacts, and I had placed some products of my alchemical talents with him on consignment from time to time.

There were several letters from Merriweather to Kavanaugh, and copies of three letters from Kavanaugh to Merriweather. Behind the letters in the file were clippings from several London newspapers. The first, published right after the previous Christmas, was about Merriweather being found dead in his shop. A story from three days later said his death had been from natural causes.

I checked the letters again and saw that the first one was dated in September the year before, and the last one was dated in early December. In that letter, Kavanaugh indicated he would soon be in London.

Back to the news clippings, and in January, a story said Scotland Yard had declared Merriweather's death a homicide from aconite poisoning.

Aconitum uncinatum, common southern monkshood, was blooming in the herb garden right outside my door. It was beautiful and one of the deadliest poisonous plants in the world. Alchemists and poisoners had used the plant for centuries.

That evening, I called Steven McCallum.

"Steve? Savanna Robinson. How's the land of the lotus eaters?"

"Savanna? Hey, good to hear from you. You know, same old, same old. Things just chugging along here in paradise. How's Wicklow? As old and stuffy as people say?"

"In many ways. Have you found a job yet?"

I heard him take a deep breath. "The Institute wants me to teach a couple of classes. Adjunct pay. It's barely enough to pay the rent, let alone eat, so I've held out. I applied for a job down in Half Moon Bay. Why?"

"Full-time staff job, Horticulture Manager. Greenhouse and herb garden, as well as the vegetable and flower gardens. Starting immediately. Probably a part-time teaching opportunity as well."

Silence, then, "No kidding?"

"No kidding. Write down this number. Dr. Jerome Carver." I went on to give him the listed number of Carver's secretary as well. After I hung up, I felt a little guilty that I hadn't mentioned the murder, but it would be good to have one familiar face around. Steve was twelve years younger than I was, but during the years he had studied under me, he had become a good friend.

CHAPTER 5

Emma showed up at my garden door the following morning, freshly scrubbed and wearing a red blouse and clean, new blue jeans. I had neglected to ask her if she was a vegetarian—so many young witches were—so I had prepared fresh fruit, yogurt, and banana nut bread straight from the oven.

The young graduate student brought two notebooks and two files stuffed with paper.

"Tell me about your background," I said as I poured tea.

"I grew up in Santa Fe, did my bachelor's in witchcraft in Boulder, and a doctor of pharmacy at the University of New Mexico. I applied here and in Sausalito for my doctoral studies in Apothecary Arts, and got accepted to both. I'd never spent much time in the east before, and I have family in the area, so I took the offer here. Dr. Kavanaugh gave me a job in the greenhouse."

I had grown up in Santa Fe, too, and would have graduated high school about the time Emma was born.

"You have a pharmacy degree?" I was surprised. I had a degree in pharmacology, but many arcane institutions took a dim view of mixing mundane medicine with magic. That prejudice was one of the reasons I never got a tenure-track job at the Sausalito Institute of Witchcraft. "It's lucky you came here. That other school doesn't care for that sort of thing."

Emma told me a little about herself and her family while we ate, and I looked through the material she brought. Her pharmacy dissertation was interesting and well done. One thing that came out of our discussion was that she was only lightly touched with the healer's gift. She had considered studying mundane medicine, but instead, opted for magical apothecary.

"Have you thought about a subject to study for your dissertation?" I asked.

"The differences and similarities between natural drugs and pharmaceuticals."

"For treating the same conditions? How are you going to find patients for such a study?"

"I was hoping at Community Hospital here. Some of the doctors are witches, and a lot of the patients are witches, also. I've spoken to Dr. Evans at the college infirmary already."

I liked her, and she was obviously bright and studious. "I'll take you on. The subject interests me as well. My father is a doctor and a healer, so he's a resource you can use. I'll put you in touch with him."

It did seem a little strange that she didn't know who my father was. He was well-known in the witchy community in Santa Fe.

Switching gears, I said, "Tell me about Dr. Kavanaugh. What was he like?"

Emma stiffened a little, looking down at her plate, squirming a bit. She took a sip of her tea.

"He was all right."

I chuckled. "That's a ringing endorsement. Hey, he's not here anymore. I took his place, though, and it kind of bothers me that whoever killed him is still out there."

With a slight shrug and a small shake of her head, Emma said, "I don't think you'll have any problems."

"Why?" I read the girl's expression and body language. "Because I'm a woman?"

Emma looked away, then said, "Maybe."

I leaned forward, an elbow on the table. "Come on, spill."

"Well, I mean, he sorta creeped me out sometimes."

"Did he hit on other girls?"

She performed a turtle-like shrug, drawing her head down to her shoulders. "Not that I saw, but there are rumors that he had breached the code. Stories about girls in the past. Lia told me that she felt sometimes like he was grooming some of the girls."

"Lia?"

"Yeah, Ophelia Harkness, the other grad student who works here. She's working on her master's, but she did her undergrad here."

"I understand there will be three undergrads working here starting next week. Do you know if any of them had any issues with him?"

Emma shook her head. "They'll all be new. None of the girls who worked here last year are coming back, except for Lia and me. None of them applied."

"No men?"

"Uh, no. As far as I know, the people who've worked in the garden and the greenhouse the past few years have all been women."

Interesting. Obviously, Emma thought Kavanaugh's killer was a woman or linked to a woman. That reminded me of something. "Dr. Carver said that students weren't allowed back on campus until yesterday. Who took care of the garden and the greenhouse this summer?"

"Mrs. Donnelly quit at the end of spring trimester, so me, mostly. Agnes came in twice a week." She gave me a sly grin. "It was kinda nice, you know? No boss, able to do things my way.

They paid me and gave me free room and board. During the summers, the only students on campus are graduate students. A lot of us have projects we can't abandon, or in my case, things I needed to grow."

"How did Dr. Kavanaugh and Agnes get along?"

Emma snorted. "Oil and water. He was extremely condescending toward her. They had a huge argument the day he was killed."

"Oh?"

"Yeah. That was Thursday morning, and they found his body the following day. He didn't show up for class, so Katy went looking for him."

"Katy?" That was the second time someone had mentioned that name.

"Dean Carver's secretary. Katy Bosun. She and Dr. Kavanaugh were friends. Shook her up pretty badly."

"Do you know what they were arguing about?"

"No, I got out of there. When witches get that mad, you never know when they might start throwing things—you know, fireballs, lightning, potted plants," she said with a grin.

I spent the rest of the morning in the greenhouse with Emma. Even if I wouldn't be working there, I needed the herbs and other botanicals for my apothecary classes.

After we broke for lunch, I called Kelly and asked her over for dinner. "Payback for Sunday night."

I heard Kelly laugh. "You don't have to do that. What time?"

I told Emma I would be gone for a while and took the bus into town where I bought fish, a few other things, and a bottle of wine. On my way back to the bus stop, I walked by a shop called Back to Basics, advertising herbs, folk remedies, and 'enchanting gifts.' I stopped and looked in the window. Inside, Agnes was arranging things on a shelf. I was in a hurry but made a note to myself to stop in sometime later.

When Kelly showed up that evening, she said, "Something smells great!" She whirled around the main room, checking out my pictures and the few knick knacks I'd placed on the fireplace mantle and the windowsills.

"We'll hope it tastes good," I replied. "Wine?"

While we ate, I told Kelly about my conversation with Emma. "You said there were a number of different theories and suspects in Kavanaugh's death. A woman perhaps?"

Kelly chuckled. "A woman is definitely involved in most of the theories. Brett was no monk."

"Do you know if he was seeing anyone?"

With a shake of her head, Kelly said, "Not anyone specific. Not anyone here, anyway, but he used to hang out at one of the pubs in town. And I know he went down to Pittsburgh a lot. The cultural scene in Wicklow is fairly limited, and Brett liked high-brow entertainments—the symphony, opera, ballet, the sorts of things student bars are rather short on."

"What about you? Did he ever hit on you?"

"Oh, yeah. Not when I was a student, though. I had him only for one class—Theory of Alchemy—when I was a freshman. When I came back here to work, however, he lost no time asking me out. But after a couple of dates, I told him I didn't think we'd be a good match."

"Any particular reason? And how did he take it?"

"Are you trying to solve his murder?" Kelly asked with a laugh. "He took it okay. He didn't say it, but the vibe I got was, 'your loss, lots of other fish out there.' As to reasons, there were several. He was a player, and I'm not into that. Very macho. I could see he liked control. And there were rumors that led me to believe I was at the top of his preferred age range. That was a little creepy."

"And he was how old?"

"Fifty. He came here twenty-five years ago. Taught at Salem before, and one of the rumors about his leaving there involved a scandal having to do with a student. He was offered the chance to resign before he was fired."

"And they hired him here?"

"Oh, I didn't hear that rumor here. A friend of my parents teaches at Salem. I called her to check on him, and she told me." Kelly sat back, swirled her wine, and took a sip. "Killed by a jilted lover? A girl he tried to seduce? Possible. The weapon used makes it look like it wasn't premeditated."

I switched topics. "Have you ever heard of Harold Merriweather?"

Kelly's demeanor changed. "Yes, such a tragedy. I was at his shop just the day before."

"In London?"

"Yes, my sister and I spent Christmas there with my grandmother. Solstice with the parents, Christmas with her. It's kind of my family tradition."

"I thought you were from DC."

"I am, but my parents are English. I was born in DC and grew up there. My Da worked for the British government—Foreign Ministry. Anyway, I dropped by to see Uncle Harold, and he took me to dinner at the Artificer's Club. Very fancy and very old-fashioned English. Have you ever been there?"

"Never had the pleasure. Uncle Harold?"

"Yes, Harold Merriweather was my mother's older brother. He seemed perfectly fine, then the next day, heart attack."

I frowned, debated with myself for a moment, then got up and went to my bedroom. When I came back, I handed Kelly the newspaper clipping about the revised cause of death.

Kelly read it, then looked up, an astonished expression on her face. "Poison? I never heard about this. Where did you get it?"

"No one cleaned out Brett Kavanaugh's office, and I found it in his desk. Tell me, do the initials GG mean anything to you?"

Kelly shook her head, still looking at the clipping,

"In connection with a rare book, perhaps?" I prodded.

"GG. Hmmm. The Gambler Grimoire? That's the only thing I can think of."

"Never heard of it."

"It's a legend. Supposedly contains spells that alter the laws of probability. You know, go to Las Vegas, cast a spell, and your dice all come up sevens."

Getting up again, I grabbed the rest of the file folder and the bottle of wine. I filled both of our glasses, then said, "Take a look at this. That clipping was in it."

I sat back and sipped my wine, watching Kelly read the letters, and then the clippings.

"He was interested in a book."

"One they both referred to as GG."

Kelly shook her head. "It's too late now, but I'll call Mom in the morning. She's over there, you know. She's been there for months—she and her sister—trying to straighten out Uncle Harold's affairs and sell the shop. It's been a nightmare, attempting to classify his inventory. When a single book can be worth tens of thousands of dollars, can you trust any expert you bring in to value it? They all want something that he had."

Kelly lay the folder down, took a sip of her wine, and said, "So, Brett possibly killed my uncle, stole a legendary book, came back here, and was bludgeoned to death by a woman he defiled. And then she took the book? Maybe she killed him for the book. Or someone else found the book after she split the scene. Oh, I love a good mystery. Let's see how many other suspects we can drag into this. How about a one-handed man with a monkey?"

CHAPTER 6

I went by Carver's office the following morning. His secretary was a smartly dressed good-looking woman a few years older than me.

"Ms. Bosun? I was wondering if I might get some boxes for Dr. Kavanaugh's stuff that's still in the office."

"Call me Katy," the woman said and pointed to where a dozen flat boxes were stacked against the wall, along with scissors, tape, and marking pens.

"You're one step ahead of me."

Katy smiled. "I try."

"Katy, no one cleaned out that office. I mean, someone dusted it, but left all his stuff. Did the police ever search it?"

The secretary looked thoughtful for a moment, then said, "I don't think so. They searched his apartment, but I never opened his office for them. The only person I ever opened it for was the custodian, the beginning of last week."

"Could someone else have gotten in there?"

"I don't think so. Brett had a key, you have the spare, and I have a master key to all the faculty offices. It's only for emergencies, you understand. Most faculty ward their offices, so even having a key normally wouldn't help anyone who wanted to get in."

I was taken back a little. "Ward their offices? Why?"

Katy smiled. "Not against ordinary criminals. The building itself, and all the buildings on campus, are warded against intruders. Outsiders have to be escorted. But students have probably wanted early access to examination questions for the past thousand years, and when your students are witches, you have to take extra precautions."

I had to laugh. "I never left exams in my office in Sausalito."

"The police did spend a week going through his apartment, though. They still won't let us clean it up."

"Someone told me you and Dr. Kavanaugh were friends."

Katy nodded. "Yes, for a long time. Twenty-six years."

"Do you know of anyone who might have wanted to harm him?"

"Other than an ex? No, not really. And if you want to know who his exes are, get a phone book and start with A."

"Ladies' man, huh?"

Katy pointed to a wall covered with people's portraits. "Second from the left in the third row."

"Tall, blond, and handsome?" I asked.

"Very handsome, charming, and a very gifted flirt with a voice that made women want to believe his sweet lies and drop their drawers. His family had money, so that didn't hurt either. He didn't need this salary."

"You and he?"

Katy shook her head. "I was a newlywed when Brett started here. I had eyes only for one man. Brett respected that. Maybe that's why we became friends—I was inaccessible."

"What about his family?"

"His father died about three or four years ago, his mother has dementia and is in a nursing home. He didn't keep in touch with his sister."

"Any idea who his heirs might be?"

Katy shook her head again. "None. He never spoke of that sort of thing. He never married, so I guess his sister."

I took the boxes down to my office in two trips, then got to work sorting through Kavanaugh's files. Some of it that I judged to be useful, such as research papers of his and others, I kept. I also kept the personal files in that bottom right desk drawer to go through for clues as to his activities. They included a lot of financial information, such as stock investments and bank accounts.

The books on the shelves were mainly academic texts. No grimoires or spell books that I wouldn't want a student to lay their hands on. That made me wonder what the bookshelves in his apartment held. But how to get in there? David Hamilton was the only person I'd seen going into any of the doors along the portico where I lived, but there were lights in most of the windows at night.

I assumed that any wards Kavanaugh might have set disappeared with his death. I looked out the window, across the Quad toward his apartment, but other buildings blocked my view. The outer door at ground level wouldn't be either warded or locked. I wondered who might live in the apartment immediately below him. For the first time, I wondered who might live in the two apartments above me.

I drew runes on my office door, placed Kavanaugh's personal files in a banker box, activated the ward, and took the box to my apartment. In contrast to the day before, there were a lot more people on campus. The students had definitely started returning.

As I walked along the breezeway between the two faculty apartment buildings, a man walked up the front stairs. He turned toward the doors on the north side, across from my entrance.

"Hello," I called as I drew even with him.

He turned from opening the door to the stairs, and I saw it was David Hamilton, the man who watched me from his window the day I arrived.

"Hello," he responded. "Dr. Robinson?" His voice was a mellow, pleasant, cultured New England baritone.

With a smile, I said, "Yes. And you're Dr. Hamilton?"

His smile wasn't openly friendly, but it was a smile. "Yes, I am. Welcome to Wicklow."

For the first time, he seemed to see the box I was carrying and quickly moved across the interval between us.

"Here, let me take that." Without waiting for my response, he snatched the box from my hands. "Hard to open the door carrying this."

We stood, the two of us looking at each other. After a few moments, I realized he was waiting for me to do something. I fished my key from my purse and turned to open the door. I dissolved the ward and pushed the door open. Hamilton was so close behind me that I couldn't easily turn around.

I stepped into the hall, and he followed, then passed me. He walked across the sitting room and set the box on the desk.

"There you go." He looked around the room. "Are you settling in?"

"Yes, but I'm not sure anyone can tell. It still looks like a man's study from eighteen-eighty."

Glancing up at the portrait over the fire place, Hamilton chuckled. "William Howard, fourth Earl of Wicklow. He was never here, you know, but he provided the seed capital for this pile of rocks. He commissioned the portrait in Ireland and shipped it over here so wayward son Robert might never forget who gave him the butter for his bread. You'll notice that this wall is as far from the mansion Robert built as you can get, and still be inside the college."

I couldn't help but laugh. "That is highly irreverent. I was told you're a conservative traditionalist."

"Oh, I am. So hidebound I can barely see past my stiff upper lip. But I was told the same tale when I was a student here, and I've never had reason to doubt it," he said with a grin.

I sighed. "I wish I didn't have him staring at me all the time, but I'm sure if I try to take it down, someone will throw a fit."

"I think it's holding the wall up," Hamilton said. "You'd be responsible for the entire college falling apart."

I couldn't believe this was the same man I had pictured as dour and judgmental as he watched me from his window.

"May I offer you something to drink? I have wine, tea, and coffee."

"No, thank you. I must be getting along. But another time, perhaps." He started toward the door but stopped and turned just before the hallway. "You know, we do have porters who haven't nearly enough to do. Next time you want to haul half the library home, call one of them to do the heavy lifting." With that, he turned and exited.

Not at all as I had envisioned him from Kelly's description.

Two streets ran between my apartment and the river, one inside the college walls that circled the campus, and one outside the walls, running north and south parallel to the river. To the north was Wicklow City, and to the south, the road eventually merged with the highway to Pittsburgh. Kelly parked her car in a lot inside the wall across the street from my place, and as a result, walked by every morning and afternoon.

An hour after Hamilton left, I answered a knock on the door to find Kelly standing there. She pulled a bottle of vodka and a bottle of cranberry juice out of her purse.

"May I come in and borrow a glass? It's been a hell of a day."

Laughing, I ushered her in and retrieved two glasses with ice from the kitchen.

"I thought libraries were quiet places. What's going on?"

"The monsters from hell have returned. Students."

"I figured they'd all be either in the pubs, or shagging each other," I said, "not in the library."

"You would think. I must have done terrible things in a past life."

She poured a third of her glass full of vodka and passed the bottle to me. I poured far less in my own glass. Kelly filled both glasses with juice and held hers up.

"Cheers."

We clinked glasses, and I took a sip. Kelly took a gulp.

"I met David Hamilton today," I said. "I was pleasantly surprised after what you said about him. I found him to be witty and rather charming."

Kelly grimaced. "I may be jaundiced. He was my professor in three classes as an undergrad, including Elemental Physics. I worked my ass off in that class to pull a three." She took another large swallow of her drink.

"You should go easy on that. You have to drive."

Kelly shook her head. "I'll take the bus, or if I'm too far gone for that, you can call the porters to carry me back to the library. I have a small room with a cot off my office. Comes in handy around finals time when students want to cram a trimester's worth of study into a few nights."

"Today can't have been that bad."

"Oh, yeah it could. Caught three kids trying to break the wards on a restricted area in the museum. A room that holds magical books and artifacts that no one wants running around free in the world. That's all we need, some idiots trying to call a demon, or reroute the Allegheny."

I laughed. "Do you know, the police never looked in Kavanaugh's office? I wonder what he has in his apartment they might have missed? If he collected rare grimoires, I'd hate for them to fall into the wrong hands."

Kelly eyed me over the rim of her glass. "What are you suggesting?"

"I'll bet the cops didn't ward his apartment. It may not even be locked. And that means students could get in there. You know they'll try. The allure of a murder scene? What we need is someone to take a look at what he had. The books, the artifacts."

In spite of Kelly eyeing me suspiciously, I ploughed on.

"Besides, Kavanaugh had no heirs, and Carver said I could have any of his books I wanted, and the rest would go to the library. His personal grimoire wasn't in his office, so unless the murderer took it, it's in his apartment. An alchemist's grimoire could be a very dangerous thing in the wrong hands. Who lives in the apartment below him?"

"Dr. Jameson, but he's never there. He basically lives with his mistress up on Hilltop Road, east of the city."

"See? There's no protection for anything in that apartment."

"So, you're saying we should just pop over there and loot the place."

"That's a very crude way of looking at it. I'm just saying that someone should inventory what's there, and anything that's possibly dangerous should be secured."

I watched her drain her glass and pour another. "You should eat something. Omelet? I have some smoked salmon."

"Sure, that sounds good. Considering that Brett died in March, students had two months before the end of term to go snooping in there. I'm not sure any of them have an attention span that would sustain their interest over the summer. Other than you, I haven't heard anyone mention Brett in months."

CHAPTER 7

No one was around, and the stairway door to Kavanaugh's apartment was unlocked, as we expected. Kelly had verified that Jameson's car wasn't in the parking lot, so once inside the stairwell, I kindled the magelights illuminating the stairs.

We passed Jameson's door at the landing, and at the top faced Kavanaugh's door with a single band of yellow police tape across it. I could see fingerprints on the doorknob that was still white with powder from the forensics investigators. I put on latex gloves, reached under the tape, turned the doorknob, and pushed. The door swung inward.

"I told you it wouldn't be locked," I whispered, ducking under the tape. Inside, I kindled a dim magelight in my palm and set it on my shoulder. Kelly did the same. The smell was most unpleasant, so I reached in my pocket for a small bottle. Pulling the stopper, I passed it under my nose, then under Kelly's nose.

"Wow. Roses. That's great. Got two of those?"

I smiled. "It won't wear off for a couple of hours."

The apartment was identical to mine, only flipped. It was far more personalized, and far more cluttered, though. The ceiling was also lower, and in Kavanaugh's apartment, instead of the wall of windows I had facing the herb garden, he had two waist-high windows overlooking the greenhouse and the countryside beyond to the south. He also had windows that overlooked Howard Quad. And, of course, there was no outside door.

That gave me a bit of a claustrophobic twinge, like I always had in my apartment in Oakland. It bothered me to be high above the ground with no fire exit.

On the floor in front of the fireplace was a large bloodstain, and the fireplace itself and the hearth were splattered with blood. A chalk line on the floor, including part of an oriental rug, showed where the body had lain.

"They'll never get that stain out now," Kelly said. "They'll have to replace the floor."

I turned to her and said, "No, I can whip something up that will draw it all out. Not a problem. The rug, not so easy, but I can make something that will do blood as well as red-wine stains."

"I need some of that."

"Well, Miss Archivist, what do you think?"

Kelly moved to the bookshelves on our left, walking slowly along, her open hand held up with her palm facing the books.

"Here," she said as she reached the end of the shelves. She started pulling books from a shelf and handing them to me. She stopped after five books, then knelt down and pulled two more off the bottom shelf. I slipped them into the tote bag I'd brought without looking at them. There would be plenty of time for that later.

Next, Kelly checked the low shelves behind the desk running under the windows. She pulled two more books from that shelf, both of which would have been in easy reach of someone sitting behind the desk. I recognized both as books of alchemical formulae that I also owned. I had seen the third book in the set in the laboratory downstairs.

Kelly turned her attention to the desk. "Nothing magical in here, but you might want to check his files. There might be something else about GG."

I nodded as Kelly moved toward the bedroom. The desk was identical to the one in Kavanaugh's office in the Administration Building, so I tried to pull open the bottom right door. As with the other one, it was locked. I bent down and sketched a rune against the lock. "*Patentibus.*"

The lock clicked. At the same time, I heard the sound of the outside door opening. Someone crept down the hall toward me, a dim magelight such as mine providing light. I killed my light and stayed crouched behind the desk until the intruder emerged from the hallway.

I slid my wand from my sleeve and my athame from the sheath on my belt, then raised up. "*Solis praeclara luce!*"

A light as bright as the sun shot from my wand, blinding the man standing there. He ducked his head and raised his arm in front of his eyes, but not before I recognized him. David Hamilton.

From the corner of my eye, I saw Kelly in the bedroom doorway, also holding a wand. The librarian pointed at Hamilton and said a Word. Hamilton froze.

I cut off the light, reflexively glancing at the windows behind me. If anyone was on the Quad, they would have seen that bright flash. I rekindled my magelight and moved around the desk toward Hamilton.

"What are you doing here?" I asked.

He stared straight ahead, hand still in front of his face, completely motionless.

"Kelly?"

The younger woman dissolved her spell, and I saw the rigidity leave Hamilton's posture.

"You could probably see that light from space. I might ask you the same question," he said. "I was coming home and noticed a glow in the window. It hasn't been there the past few months, so I was curious."

"Dr. Carver said that I could have Dr. Kavanaugh's books," I said. "I came to see what was here."

Hamilton chuckled. "Don't you think it would be easier to see them with the lights on? Or maybe even in daylight? Of course, I'm sure you notified the police you were coming."

"I caught students trying to break into a restricted area at the museum today," Kelly said. "We thought there might be things in here they shouldn't have, so we checked, and the door wasn't even locked."

"Ah. That makes all kinds of sense," Hamilton said. "Did you find anything too dangerous for them?"

Kelly hesitated, and I glanced her way.

"I think he kept his grimoire in the bedroom," Hamilton said. "He had a spelled box."

Kelly crooked her finger. "I think you need to see this."

"What is it?" I asked as I sheathed my knife and tucked the wand back into its sheath fastened to my forearm inside my sleeve. I motioned Hamilton to precede me, and with a slight bow of his head and a quirky grin, he followed Kelly into the bedroom.

An intricately carved box of reddish wood—more than two feet square and a foot deep—sat open on the bed. Inside were four books, a necklace, and a small figurine. I leaned close, shining my light on the contents, then gasped.

I'm sure the chill that passed over me, the sinking feeling in my stomach, were psychological, but the contents of that box scared me.

"Well, that certainly lends some credibility to your story for being here," Hamilton said. I thought his voice sounded a little shaky.

The book on the right was covered in some kind of leather. The black lettering said, '*Maleficium Spiritus*'—Evil Spirits—possibly the most notorious book of black magic in the Western world. Magic could be felt emanating from it, and it wasn't a warm, cozy feeling.

"I'll bet it's the real thing," Kelly said. Her voice was definitely shaky. "I think the cover is human skin, and the lettering is painted in human blood. The book next to it, I think, is Brett's grimoire. I haven't touched either of them, so I'm not sure what those books underneath are."

"The necklace is a voodoo protection charm," Hamilton said. "Not exactly harmless. Voodoo tends to think of offense as the best defense. Attack someone wearing it, and it will strike back."

"And the statuette?" I asked.

Kelly shrugged. "No idea. Looks Middle Eastern. I'd have to study it, compare what I find to what I have in the database." She passed her hand over the artifact. "It does have some kind of power."

She turned and pointed to a much larger statuette on the dresser, about two or three feet tall. "That, I recognize. A *nkisi nkondi*, a power statue from central Africa. It's used as a tracking device by witch hunters." Kelly looked at Hamilton. "Did you know he collected such exotic toys?"

Hamilton shook his head. "I knew he collected." He swung his hand toward the other room. "If you look around, you'll see a lot of stuff, but not this kind of thing. I've never been in his bedroom before."

"Have you ever heard of the Gambler Grimoire?" I asked.

He snorted a laugh. "Sure, who hasn't? A myth. I've seen a couple of spells purportedly taken from it. I wasn't impressed."

"We think Dr. Kavanaugh considered it as more than a myth," I said. "So, do you want us to leave all this here, close the door, and tell the police that we think someone should nuke the place? Or what?"

He licked his lips, then shook his head. "No, we should clear it out of here. You have secure storage for this, don't you?"

"Yes," Kelly said. "At the museum, if we can keep students out of it. What do I tell Carver and Phillips? I can't just stash this sort of thing in the museum and pretend it floated in through the window. You do know Dr. Phillips's talents."

Hamilton took a deep breath, staring down at the box on the bed.

"The president, Dr. Phillips, is an archivist and archeologist, as well as a historian. Magically, he's a librarian," Kelly told me. "He's my direct boss, and I can't take something like *this book* into the museum without telling him. It would be my job."

"Not to mention having to explain how we found it," Hamilton said. "I, for one, am not very keen on telling Dr. Carver or Sam Kagan about this little midnight foray."

"We can stash it in my place until we figure out what to do with it," I said. I looked around, then turned to Hamilton. "You've been here long enough that I imagine you've managed to fill up your space."

"Or," Kelly said, "don't you have an alchemist's safe in your lab? That would be as secure as what I have at the museum."

I nodded. "Yes, and it has plenty of room. Before I looked in it, I don't think it had been opened since Dr. Kavanaugh died."

"Well, we know that whoever killed him wasn't looking for this," Hamilton said.

Kelly pursed her lips and shook her head. "Not necessarily. I'm not sure either of you would have found this box. The spells on it were, shall we say, unusual, and quite complex."

"How close were you and Dr. Kavanaugh?" I asked Hamilton.

He shrugged. "Fairly close. We've been working together for

more than twenty years, lived right across the breezeway from each other. We took a couple of vacations together when we were younger, but our tastes for certain things diverged as we got older."

The three of us made another pass through the suite, searching for more books or items of interest. I was the unfortunate one who opened the refrigerator, quickly closing it. Even the rose oil wasn't enough to completely block the stench.

"Whew. No one even bothered to clean out his fridge. It looks and smells like a biology student's nightmare."

Hamilton raised an eyebrow when I gathered the files from the desk.

"I'll tell you later," I said.

It was almost midnight by the time I sealed the grimoire box, other books, and the artifacts we found into the alchemist's safe in the lab. We trooped back to my apartment, where we poured ourselves another drink. Hamilton took his without the cranberry juice.

I pulled out the GG file I'd taken from Kavanaugh's office and handed it to Hamilton.

"No one cleaned out his office. I found this in his desk."

After fifteen minutes, he put the file folder on the table. "So, you think this is about the Gambler Grimoire?"

I shrugged. "He was interested in some rare book coded GG."

"And you suspect Brett might have killed Harold Merriweather to get it."

Again, I shrugged. "Everyone I've talked to seems to think Kavanaugh was killed by a jealous lover or ex-lover. This is another theory. What bothers me is that the police didn't even investigate his death very thoroughly. Suppose we have some madman running around with a hatred of alchemists? That would put me square in the crosshairs. I just want to know what happened so I know if I'm safe or not."

"That's reasonable," he said. "Although, judging from tonight, you're quite capable of taking care of yourself."

"I'm sure Brett Kavanaugh thought he was, too, until someone brained him from behind. I had hoped we might find a computer tonight, since there wasn't one in his office. There was a printer in both places."

"Really?" Hamilton looked surprised. "He had a fancy new laptop he gave himself for Christmas. Maybe the police have it."

CHAPTER 8

The following morning, I dragged myself out of bed, took a shower, then woke Kelly, who was sleeping on my couch. I made breakfast while Kelly showered, then walked with her as far as the Administration Building.

At Carver's office, I spoke to Katy. "I have a bunch of Dr. Kavanaugh's stuff boxed up. Can you please have a porter take it to wherever you want to store it?"

"Yes, I'll call the porter service and have it taken care of."

"One other thing. What about the books in his apartment? Is there any way I could take a look at them?"

She looked thoughtful. "I don't know. No one's been in there, that I know of. I think the police still have the apartment sealed off."

"No one? No one's cleaned the place? It's been five months, Katy." I put on a surprised expression. "I don't know much about how the police handle this sort of thing, but did they empty his refrigerator?"

Katy leaned forward, her brow furrowed, then her eyes popped wide. "Oh, my. I'll call Lieutenant Kagan."

She reached for the phone while I waited.

"Lieutenant? This is Katy Bosun in Dr. Carver's office at the college. Have you finished with Dr. Kavanaugh's apartment? Yes, we would like to get some things from it, and get it cleaned, you know. We do have a waiting list for apartments in that building. Uh huh. Uh huh. All right, thank you. And, oh, do you know if anyone cleaned out the refrigerator?"

When she hung up, she said, "He said he'll be right over. My word, if no one's cleaned up, how are we ever going to get the blood...there was so much blood."

I reached over, patted her hand, and gave her a comforting smile. "I'm an alchemist. I can mix up a cleaning solution that will pull blood out of a turnip. I can also give your cleaner something that will fix the odors."

"Oh, that would be wonderful. Thank you, Dr. Robinson."

"Savanna, please."

Katy grinned and winked at me. "Not at work, but I'd be pleased to call you Savanna outside of work hours." Her eyes flicked toward the inner door to Carver's office. "Decorum, you know."

"So, you can't think of anyone who didn't get along with Dr. Kavanaugh?" I asked.

"Oh, there were people he didn't get along with, I imagine. Brett could be rather pompous and condescending. But hate him enough to kill him? Not that I know of." Katy shrugged. "I think that's why most people think it was one of his lovers. The problem is figuring out who he was bedding that week."

"Who were his friends?"

"Here at the college? Me, David Hamilton. He used to be close to Anton Ricard, but some years ago he and David and Anton had a falling out. Over a woman, of course. But that was what, ten, twelve years ago? And she left Wicklow that long ago. He'd been here long enough to have quite a few friends in town and in Pittsburgh."

"A love quadrangle?" I said with a smirk.

Katy grinned. "Something like that. I got the impression that she liked all three men, but didn't love any of them."

After leaving Katy, I walked over to my lab. The cleaning solution and the air freshener took me about an hour to whip up. Then I went up to Kavanaugh's apartment. The door was still as I had left it the previous night, with a paper match closed in the door. Satisfied that Lieutenant Kagan had not arrived yet, I went downstairs and sat on my stoop to wait for him. He would have to pass me to reach Kavanaugh's place.

I was daydreaming when a voice, very close, asked, "Are you locked out?"

Looking up at David Hamilton, I said, "No, waiting for the police. Katy called them about Kavanaugh's apartment. Do you know what Lieutenant Kagan looks like?"

His face twisted into a half-grin. "He looks like a cop. Flattop haircut, about five-ten, thirty or forty pounds overweight. Smart, though. I think he feels the people here at the college are stonewalling him, because he can't find anything he can grab onto. I know how he feels, but I think it's because there isn't much. What you found the past couple of days, well, he probably should have that. Enjoy."

And with that, he walked off and entered the stairwell to his apartment. I waited, and about five minutes later spotted him in his window. I smiled and waved, he frowned and disappeared. A difficult man to figure out.

So far, I had made friends with Kelly, and Katy seemed like someone I'd enjoy spending time with, but she was married with kids and grandkids. A male friend would be nice.

When a man fitting Kagan's description, wearing an ill-fitting cheap suit, trotted up the outside steps, I stood. As he passed, I called out to him.

"Lieutenant Kagan?"

He stopped and turned toward me. "Yes?"

"Hi. I'm Dr. Savanna Robinson. Katy asked me to meet you here."

"Oh? Well, shall we?"

He started off toward Kavanaugh's, and I fell in beside him.

Kagan was scoping me out from the corner of his eye. "I don't remember speaking to you when I was investigating the case."

"I've been here five days. I'm Dr. Kavanaugh's replacement. Dr. Carver said he didn't have any family, no heirs that they know of, so he said I could have his books. I wanted some of the ones I found in his office, but I wondered what he might have at home. Katy said I'd have to ask the police if I could go in."

We walked a little farther. "His office?"

"Yes, in the Administration Building. All the professors have offices there."

When we reached the door, Kagan pulled it open and stood aside so I could go first.

"No one told me he had an office apart from this one. I thought this was his office."

"Nope. I've been told that most of the faculty live off campus. We all have offices away from our living quarters."

We trudged up the stairs, and I arrived at the top while a panting Kagan was a flight below me. I wondered if the climb was part of what discouraged him from investigating more thoroughly. I hadn't seen an elevator anywhere at the college. The fact he hadn't known about Kavanaugh's office made me wonder how competent Kagan was. He didn't seem to have asked some very basic questions.

While I waited for him, I took a sniff of the magic-infused rose oil.

Kagan arrived and pulled a set of keys from his jacket pocket, sorted through them until he found the one he wanted, and opened the door.

"Do you always lock the door?" I asked.

"Of course."

"Are those Dr. Kavanaugh's keys?"

He blinked at me, looked down at the keys in his hand, then back to me. "Yes, why?"

"Well, I'm his replacement. I don't have a key to my desk, or my office. I have to ask Katy to open it for me," I lied.

"Oh. Yes, well, I'll see what I can do."

No keys and no promise. I hoped he solved the case before I retired.

"It is a little ripe in here," he said, skirting the bloodstain on the floor to open the windows across the room.

"If no one has cleaned out that refrigerator, I'll bet it's more than ripe."

He took the bait, walking into the kitchen and opening the appliance in question. He slammed it shut even quicker, gagging, and then running to the window and sticking his head out. Taking pity on him, I walked over beside him and held out the rose oil.

"Take a sniff. It'll help."

Kagan took the bottle and gingerly passed it under his nostrils. His eyes widened, and he inhaled deeply.

"Thanks," he said, handing the bottle back. "Normally, the police don't clean up crime scenes, but I can give you a number the college can call."

"Normally, do you keep yellow tape across the door for five months?"

His face reddened. "In my defense, I got pulled onto another case. A drug dealer came up from Pittsburgh and had a shootout with a biker gang a few days after this happened."

As we walked through the apartment, I pumped him a little more.

"All I can get out of anyone is that he had no enemies," Kagan said, "and everyone's best bet is jealous lover, jealous husband, or ex-lover. But with no physical evidence, I don't even know where to start. Look, I liked Brett, but I can't just question everyone who ever met him hoping one of them confesses."

I handed him the folder. Kelly had photocopied it all, so it wasn't a loss. Kagan sat down in a chair and spent half an hour reading it all. When he finished, he raised his head to look at me.

"Something I can't do," I said, "is check to see if he actually went to England. Was he in London on December twenty-eighth?"

Kagan shook his head. "Can I keep this?"

I shrugged. "I found it in a desk drawer in his office. I was surprised you hadn't found it. But as to the books, and other stuff," I said, waving at the pictures on the wall, figurines on the mantle, and other personal items, "Dr. Carver said he didn't have any family, no will, and no heirs. We haven't found his computer either. We wondered if you have it."

"No computer. I thought that was strange. As for the other stuff, no will, and no indications of any family. We found bank and brokerage accounts, and his retirement account. A couple of those had a named beneficiary."

I raised my eyebrows expectantly.

"I shouldn't—"

I pointedly looked at the folder in his hand.

With a deep sigh, he said, "I guess it can't hurt. The beneficiary of the retirement account is Katy Bosun, and the brokerage account beneficiary is the Wicklow College endowment fund."

"How much?"

"About half a mil to Mrs. Bosun, two-and-a-half million to the college."

I waited.

He curled his lip at me, but continued. "Almost a quarter mil in the bank. And that Jaguar parked across the street is worth a cool sixty or seventy grand. He wasn't hurting."

I looked around the room at the sculptures, artifacts, and paintings. "Dr. Hamilton said Kavanaugh was a collector. I wonder how much some of this might be worth."

CHAPTER 9

I spent that evening going through all the files I had pulled from Kavanaugh's two desks. There were receipts for more than two dozen paintings, artifacts, and books that totaled almost a million dollars. Five books of the arcane from Merriweather's ranged from three thousand to twenty-five thousand dollars each. One of the paintings had cost him a quarter of a million dollars. I reflected on my lack of art knowledge, because I hadn't seen anything in his apartment that I found that attractive.

Other files detailed his finances and verified what Kagan had told me. Two documents of interest—one twenty-five years old and the other twelve years old—were settlements, releases of liability, and promises not to sue from lawyers in exchange for fifty thousand dollars on the first one to a Rebecca Hall, and thirty-five thousand on the second to someone named Seanan Murphy. Both had been filed with the county court there in Wicklow. Both had strict non-disclosure attached to the payments. I wondered if Kagan could get into those cases.

I set aside those documents I wanted Kelly to copy for me, and the rest I put in banker boxes for Kagan. He probably wouldn't be happy I'd taken them in the first place, but more than half of all the files contained professional research and scholarly papers Kavanaugh had either written or reviewed for other scholars. Easy enough to make the case that I had a professional interest in those, and returned the others.

Katy had told me that about half the students were back on campus, with the other half expected by the end of the weekend. I didn't have a lot else to do. The courses I was assigned were some I had taught at other colleges. I had checked out the lab supplies I needed for the first trimester. I could go out and hit the bars, but nothing Kelly had told me about any of them excited me.

"So, what did you do for fun in San Francisco?" Kelly asked when she dropped by on Friday evening.

"I like music—nightclubs, concerts, outdoor venues in nice weather—Broadway road shows, theater," I said. "Great places to eat, although the food I've had here is pretty good."

"Pittsburgh for music. Exercise?"

I laughed. "Oh, you consider exercise fun? I had a gym membership, and went at least once a week to work out and swim. I did try the pool here yesterday. The Institute in Sausalito didn't have the kind of facilities we have here. I didn't own a car, so I rode my bike a lot. I sold it before I came here, though. There's only so much you want to haul with you. Why?"

I planned to go kayaking with some friends tomorrow. Would you like to come?"

"And, where would I get a kayak? Not to mention, I've never been in one in my life."

"Oh, that's not a problem. One of the guys is an instructor, and he has a couple of extra boats. I can call and ask if he minds me bringing a novice."

And that's what happened. Up at the crack of dawn, I allowed myself to be dragged down to the river north of the city, stuffed into a floating sausage casing, handed a double-ended paddle, and pushed out into a river that was moving far faster than I was expecting. By the time we pulled the kayaks out of the water for lunch and beer, I was sore in muscles I didn't realize I had.

I did have to admit that it was fun, and I met some pleasant people. It was mid-afternoon when Kelly and I got back to town.

"I discovered this morning that I need shampoo," I said as we drove in. "Can we stop somewhere?"

"No problem. I have a few things I'd like to pick up as well."

Kelly found a parking place on Main Street, a block from a grocery store that had a pharmacy.

As we got out of the car, Kelly asked, "Do you ski?"

"Why would I want to do that? I hate cold weather."

"It's fun," Kelly said, laughing.

I stopped. "Are you trying to kill me? If you can't drown me, you're going to push me off a mountain into a tree?"

Kelly laughed even harder.

As we walked down the street to the grocery store, we passed Agnes's shop. Glancing in the window, I saw a bookshelf had fallen, spilling its contents across the floor. I stopped, and took a good look. A chair was overturned, a table used to display potions and small knickknacks had been also overturned. Glancing at the front door, I saw it was ajar, but the sign hanging there said, 'Closed.'

"What the—" I walked over to the door and cautiously pushed it open.

"Agnes?" I called out.

"What's the matter?" Kelly asked coming up behind me and peering over my shoulder. "Oh. Not good."

We pushed into the shop, where there had obviously been some sort of disturbance. Making our way around the stuff littering the floor, we found Agnes on the other side of the bookcase. Lying on her stomach in a pool of blood with an athame lying next to her and her open eyes staring at infinity, she was obviously dead.

I stepped back, unable to tear my eyes away, and fumbled for the phone in my pocket.

"I'll check out the back," Kelly said, moving toward the back of the store, her wand in her hand.

"Yeah," I answered, dialing the number Kagan had given me. "Lieutenant Kagan? This is Savanna Robinson. Do you know where Back to Basics is on Main Street? Well, I think you should get down here. Agnes Bishop has been murdered."

"Don't touch anything, and stay outside," Kagan said. "I'll have someone there in a couple of minutes." He hung up.

"Kelly?" I called. "Kagan said for us to wait outside."

I waited a couple of minutes before Kelly emerged from the back.

"Someone tossed the place," she said. "I don't know what they were looking for, but the backroom has been searched. I went upstairs, and it's a total mess. I think they went out the back, the door was wide open."

I shook my head. "Agnes was a neat freak. Everything had to be just so."

We went outside, and in less than a minute, a police car, lights flashing, screeched to a halt in front of the store. Two cops got out, their hands on holstered sidearms.

"Are you the ones who called in?" the driver asked.

"Yeah," I answered, pointing to the door.

The cops went in, and through the window Kelly and I

could see them check Agnes's body, then search through the rest of the shop.

"What's upstairs?" I asked.

"She lived up there. Living room and kitchen on the next floor, and a couple of bedrooms and a bathroom on the top floor. Her workshop and a small shower room are back there," Kelly said, pointing down the hall away from the customer area of the shop.

After about five minutes, one of the cops came out just as Kagan pulled up in an unmarked car. The uniformed officer walked over to meet him, and they talked for a few minutes. Then the uniform went to his car, opened the trunk, and started pulling things out of it. Kagan walked over to us.

"What happened?"

"We were walking to the grocery store," Kelly said. "I parked over there. Savanna looked in the window."

Kagan stepped past us and took a look through the window for himself. "Okay. And then?"

"The door was open, but the sign said closed," I said. "I was by here the other day, and everything in that shop was so neat it looked like a picture in a magazine. So, we went in, and found her."

"What did you touch?" Kagan asked.

"Nothing with our hands. I pushed the door open with my shoulder. I didn't need to check if she was breathing." I leaned closer and dropped my voice. "Lieutenant Kagan, I have a healer's Gift. You wouldn't want me operating on you, but anyone with a hint of the Gift would know there wasn't anyone alive in there."

He nodded. "You're a talented woman."

I snorted. "If I was more talented, I'd be a doctor like my father instead of an apothecary. We all have a variety of abilities, don't we?"

The cop came over, handed Kagan some gloves and shoe covers, then started stringing his yellow tape across the front of the building. Kagan donned the coverings, then ducked under the tape, and went inside. The cop finished taping off the front of the shop, then ran the tape from one end of the building to a parking meter, across a couple of more, then back to the other end of the building, blocking off the sidewalk in front of the shop as well. He took the roll of tape and went inside. Looking through the window, we could see him walk down the hall, and out the back door into the alley.

A white van marked 'Crime Scene Investigation' pulled up, and four people in white coveralls, gloves, shoe covers, hats, and masks got out and went inside. Kagan came out about ten minutes later.

He handed us each some latex gloves and shoe covers. "If you don't mind, I'd like you to come inside with me."

I did mind. I had no desire to go back in there and see what remained of Agnes, but I took a deep breath, put on the shoe covers and gloves, and followed Kagan.

The woman's body still lay where we'd found her. A man was taking pictures of her from all angles. When he finished, a woman with a tag on her overalls that said 'Medical Examiner' came over and inspected Agnes, touching her in several places.

"How long?" Kagan asked.

"Less than an hour," the woman replied, touching the blood pool with one finger. "It's still liquid."

I felt a little disoriented. Kelly and I had found the body approximately thirty-five minutes before. That meant we had just missed the killer, especially since I assumed the search upstairs happened after Agnes was dead.

After the ME completed her examination, she called two of the white-clad men to turn the body over. When they did, everyone gasped. The middle of Agnes's chest was charred, and her shirt was scorched around the edges of the burn.

"What the hell?" Kagan asked.

The ME looked up at Kagan, her eyes flicking toward Kelly and me in question.

"They're from the college," Kagan said.

The ME looked back down at the body. "I don't think this was caused by anything natural."

"Fireball, perhaps," I said, "but more likely a lightning bolt. Very tight, not diffused."

A nod from the ME, then she looked at the wound that caused all the bleeding. "I'll have to verify, but that knife could be the weapon used to cut her throat." The athame in the blood pool hadn't been moved.

"The lightning bolt didn't kill her, so he used the athame to finish her," I said.

"He?" Kagan shot me a look.

"Or she. A five-foot woman could have done it as easily as a football player," I answered. "If I can get a picture of that athame, I'll show it to the ladies who work in the greenhouse."

Kagan frowned. "And you think they might recognize it?"

"If it's Agnes's, yes. My grad students worked with her in the greenhouse all last year."

He nodded. "I can send a picture to your phone."

"That works. Can I get it without all the blood?"

Kagan questioned us for another half hour, thankfully outside. When he let us go, Kelly started back toward her car.

"Hey," I called. "I still need shampoo, and I feel like I need a shower and to wash my hair even more than I did an hour ago."

We went on to the grocery store but walked back to the car afterward on the other side of the street. Neither of us wanted to get close to the crime scene again. It was a quiet drive back to my apartment.

CHAPTER 10

Kelly stopped by for a cup of coffee in the morning, then went on to the library while I gathered what I wanted to take to my office. It was registration day, when students received their class schedules, bought their books and supplies, and took care of any administrative tasks they might have. Formal classes would start on Tuesday.

I had a meeting with the students working in the garden and the greenhouse scheduled at nine o'clock, and a meeting with the graduate students I would be advising at three o'clock. In between, there was the lunch meeting with the Alchemy Department. From experience at other places I had taught, I knew I should check with the bookstore to ensure they had all the books and supplies I had ordered for my students. I also hoped to find and meet the other professors in my departments.

The girls who showed up at the nine o'clock meeting made me feel old. If I was honest with myself, Kelly made me feel old, and she was six years older than Emma. Ophelia was twenty-two but didn't appear any older than the undergrads. It felt like the students got younger every year, but I had a sneaking suspicion that I might be getting older.

I couldn't help but compare Ophelia with Kelly. If Kavanaugh was attracted to both young women, they couldn't be any different physically. Ophelia had short, dark-brown hair, and dark eyes in a round, plain face. No one would ever call her beautiful. Whereas Kelly was tall and slender, Ophelia was barely five feet tall and round, almost chubby. Emma was much more like Kelly, except for their hair color.

I asked each girl about their experience and their college major, then told them what I expected of them. I outlined the duties of the job and a general sketch of how I wanted things done. The younger girls, Ava, Charlotte, and Barbara, listened mostly with wide eyes, looking a little frightened and unsure of themselves.

"We are hoping to hire a permanent greenhouse and garden manager," I said, "but until then, Emma will be in charge and will set schedules. Make sure to give her your class schedules, and to let her know if something happens and you can't show up on time." I pointed toward my backdoor at the far end of the herb garden. "If you need me for anything, knock there. If I'm not in, try my office in the Admin Building, or leave a message with Emma or Mrs. Bosun."

The mundane wasn't what drew the questions, though. I should have expected the students would mainly be interested in other things.

"Is it true that Ms. Bishop was killed this weekend?" Emma asked.

"Yes, I'm afraid so."

I handed out copies of my class schedule, including my office hours and tutorials, then left them to organize themselves while I went to my apartment to change into appropriate professional clothing.

The rest of the day went fairly smoothly. When I got back

to my apartment, I saw Lieutenant Kagan out in the herb garden with the graduate students I was assigned to tutor.

I opened my back door and called, "Lieutenant? Are you looking for me?"

Kagan walked over to the foot of the stairs and pulled a piece of paper from his pocket. When he turned it to me, I saw it was a picture of an athame. "You said some of your students might be able to identify this?"

I took it and descended to the garden level. "Perhaps. Emma, Lia, can you come over here, please?"

The two students walked over, and I handed the picture to Emma. "Do you recognize this?"

"Yeah, it's Agnes's," Emma said and glanced at Ophelia. "Isn't it?"

The color drained out of Ophelia's face, and her hand shook as she pointed to the picture.

"Uh huh. See the mark on the pommel? She said it was passed down through her family."

"Is that how she died?" Emma asked.

Kagan reached out and took the picture. "It was found at the scene. Thanks. Do you know if she had a grimoire? We didn't find one at her shop."

"Oh, yeah," Emma said. "Old family hand-me-down. It's not here at the college, I can guarantee it. She always carried it here and took it home with her. Wouldn't let anyone touch it."

Kagan thanked them, and I walked with him toward the gate.

"I read through what you gave me," Kagan said. "Aconite? I take it that's a rather exotic poison."

"It's not commonly used," I said, "but it's not hard to find. See those tall, pretty blue flowers over there? That's aconite, also known as monkshood."

"And you have it growing here?"

I laughed at his astounded expression. "It's a native wildflower. You can probably find it growing in any undisturbed meadow between here and the Gulf of Mexico. The poison is an easy extraction that any alchemy or chemistry student could do. The entire plant is poisonous. Nasty to play with and requires caution. A couple of drops in a cup of tea would kill someone. It's not the poison I would choose, but it would do the trick."

After Kagan left, I set up appointments with each of the graduate students to discuss their interests, then sent them on their way and went to my apartment, letting myself in through the garden door. After checking the cupboard and the refrigerator, I ruefully saw that another grocery trip was needed. And for that, I either had to catch a bus, beg a ride, or call a taxi. The smartest thing to do, I decided, was to buy a new bicycle so I had transportation.

After checking the telephone book for bicycle stores, I changed clothes and caught the bus into town. The first store I went to didn't have anything I was interested in, but a woman at the second store understood what I wanted. It would have to be ordered, however.

The bus ride home with two bags of groceries wasn't much fun, but at least I would have breakfast in the morning. By the time I put the food away, I was tired and not in the mood to cook. I also had the President's reception to attend, so I decided to give the Faculty Club a try. Kelly had told me it was one of the top three restaurants in town.

I'd asked Katy earlier that day about what to wear for the reception and hadn't received a very clear answer. The Institute hadn't held many formal events. I had a knee-length coral cocktail dress and a floor-length green evening gown, either of which could be acceptable. The reception would be my first meeting with Dr. Phillips, so I decided to take a risk on being overdressed. Besides, the long dress showed off my figure better, and Phillips was single. As my mother always said, you never got a second chance to make a first impression.

After a quick shower, I put my hair up in a French twist, made an attempt at makeup, slipped the evening gown over my head, grabbed the matching heels, and headed for the door.

Walking through the quads in the long dress, with the old buildings looming above me, made me feel as though I'd been transported into a gothic novel. I cast a glance at Brett Kavanaugh's rooms as I passed them and decided that, unfortunately, it was a murder mystery, instead of a romance.

"Are you alone, Dr. Robinson?" the maître d' asked when I entered the dining room.

"Yes, and rather in a hurry, I'm afraid. The President's reception, you know."

He gave me a beatific smile. "Of course. This way, please."

We were halfway across the room when we passed Anton Ricard sitting alone at a table for two.

"Dr. Robinson. Good evening. Are you dining alone?" he asked.

"Yes, I just arrived. I had a late appointment."

Jumping to his feet, Ricard circled the table and pulled out the other chair. "Please join me."

Not wanting to seem rude, I sat down. "Thank you."

The maître d' handed me a menu, poured wine in my glass from the bottle in a cooler next to the table, and said, "I'll send the waiter over."

"I recommend the steaks, or the sea bass special tonight is wonderful," Ricard said.

I glanced at his plate, and the fish did look tempting. "I've found that the fish selection in the shops here is rather limited," I said. "Coming from San Francisco, I'm used to a bit more variety."

He chuckled. "We are a ways from the coast, and the nearest major airport is Pittsburgh. By the time seafood makes its way here, it's not exactly fresh any longer. If you're buying at the grocery, best look for frozen."

After I ordered, I took a look around the room. My dress didn't appear to be out of step with those of other women who were dining there.

"You look very elegant this evening," Ricard said.

"Thank you. I wasn't able to get a very good sense of what might be appropriate," I said. "I decided that more conservative would be safer."

Ricard laughed. "At Wicklow, conservative is never out of style." He was wearing traditional black tie and a cummerbund.

"The Institute—whether in Sausalito or Santa Cruz—was almost never very formal," I said. "I always wore a business suit in the classroom, but some professors lectured in jeans and Birkenstocks."

"Carver would have a stroke," Ricard said, "and Dr. Phillips would probably call you in for a chat."

I chuckled. "It doesn't seem as though the formality extends to the students, however."

He shook his head. "That all broke down starting in the sixties, I understand. The students here are indistinguishable from those at other universities in the area. Of course, the big upheaval came in nineteen twenty."

"When they admitted women for the first time?"

"Yes. Half the faculty resigned."

"I'm afraid that among certain groups, Wicklow's reputation is still somewhat tainted by that era," I said. The Institute of Witchcraft, where I did my doctoral studies and taught on the West Coast, was founded by women in the late nineteenth century, and the original student body was predominantly female.

Ricard laughed. "Yes, the suffragettes have still never forgiven us our patriarchal past."

"But," I said, "in some ways, Wicklow is remarkably forward-thinking. The range of subjects taught in the mundane sciences is far greater than the offerings in Sausalito."

He nodded. "I don't see how you can ignore physics and chemistry. Without such foundations, how do you teach the interactions of magic with the physical realm? I think you'll find that the prerequisite courses for upper-level alchemy have adequately prepared your students."

CHAPTER 11

When I finished my dinner, Ricard escorted me through Scholars' Quad, and on to Howard House, the home of the college president. It was lit up, and all the people in formal dress outside gave it an old-fashioned feeling. I felt sure that Robert Howard would have been comfortable if he had shown up.

When we approached Phillips, he was talking with Kelly near the main entrance. She spoke to him, and he turned toward me.

"Dr. Robinson! So nice to see you. I apologize that we haven't had a chance to chat, but I've been out of town. Ms. Grace has been telling me that you've had an unusual introduction to Wicklow."

"That's one way of putting it," I responded. "I didn't expect it to be quite so exciting."

"Hopefully it won't continue that way," Phillips said. His hope and mine were in sync. I didn't mind excitement but preferred a different sort of events.

I had seen pictures of Dr. Phillips but was surprised at how young he was. Fifty at the oldest, by my estimate. He and Ricard greeted each other like old friends, and standing together, dressed the same way, they were remarkably alike—close to the same age, same height, with the same build and dark hair.

Ricard escorted me around the room, introducing me to far more people than I could possibly remember. The ballroom was ornately decorated in typical nineteenth century fashion, and I found that far more interesting than memorizing names and faces.

It did surprise me that Kelly spent most of the evening hanging around with President Phillips. I mentioned it to Ricard.

"Oh, Ms. Grace is the President's protégé," he said with a leering note in his voice. "He actually held her position prior to his elevation. Their magical talents are very similar, and both are single, so she routinely attends him at functions when he needs an escort."

Some time later, we encountered David Hamilton. The interaction between him and Ricard was not exactly cordial, and I considered the college's internal politics and how I might fit in. Academia had a centuries-long reputation for being a snake pit of jealousy, sabotage, and back-stabbing. As a student and an instructor, I had been in Sausalito for almost a decade, and knew where the skeletons were hidden, the land mines planted, who was sleeping with whom, and who not to turn my back on.

Judging from my first few days at Wicklow, turning my back might be far more dangerous than I had ever worried about in California.

Could petty politics be the reason for Kavanaugh's murder? I couldn't see it as having anything to do with Agnes's death, however. As an adjunct instructor, she was at the lowest level in the hierarchy. Unless she was blackmailing someone. I hadn't thought about blackmail in regard to Kavanaugh, but perhaps? What were those court settlements with local women about?

"Dr. Carver told me that it had been twenty years since the last faculty murder here," I said to Ricard. "Was that killing ever solved?"

He chuckled and gave me a wink. "That was a mage duel, with a hundred witnesses in the middle of Scholars' Quad. Very good theater mixed with some fairly bad magic. A graduate student attacked a faculty member who downgraded her. In the end, she proved more competent than he was, not that it did her any good. The Council convicted her of murder, and I guess, threw her in a dungeon somewhere."

"A woman scorned?" I suggested.

"Yes, there was that rumor also," Ricard replied. "Trying to sleep your way to the top can be a risky endeavor."

"Do you have experience in that?" I asked.

He choked, and for a second, I thought he might spew his drink. Then he grinned.

"I never had the opportunity, but I had a professor as an undergrad who sparked some fantasies." His eyes traveled from my shoes up to meet my eyes. I had received such lewd compliments many times and refused to blush.

"That rumor starts anytime a young woman shows any promise," I said.

He glanced toward where Kelly was standing with Dr. Phillips. "I guess it does."

By ten o'clock, the crowd had shrunk by half, and those who were left were trickling out the door. I found Dr. Phillips and said my good night.

As I took my leave, I asked Kelly, "Are you driving?"

"Oh, no. I'll call a taxi. I've been to these things before, and I always overdo it, so I left my car at home."

To my surprise, both Hamilton and Ricard were waiting for me in the lobby, although they weren't standing together. Both started toward me when I appeared.

"Do you live here on campus?" I asked Ricard as I strolled through Scholars' Quad between the men.

"Oh, no. I have a place outside of town," he said. "You'll have to come see it sometime. I renovated an old barn, and it's quite lovely."

Hamilton was very quiet, not joining in the conversation as I asked questions about the town and the surrounding area.

The moon was very bright, illuminating the quad and casting shadows that gave the buildings an even more creepy, gothic look. As we reached the west end of the quad, I saw a dark lump in the grass near an ancient oak by the faculty dining room. It was one of the few features breaking up the smooth lawn.

"Is that someone?" I asked.

"One of the hazards of being out late at night is tripping over drunken students," Ricard replied. Indeed, we could hear shouts of revelry from the direction of the dorms and the student pub. "Attendance in your courses tomorrow morning will give you a good idea of which students are serious and which aren't."

I peered closer, and it seemed as though the person lying there was sprawled in a very uncomfortable position. I stopped, then stepped off the sidewalk in that direction. My heels sank into the moist ground, so I stripped off my shoes.

When I reached the boy, my nose told me that drunkenness wasn't his problem. My healer's Gift also told me that I needn't bother checking on his well-being. I pulled my phone from my clutch and hit one of the few contacts I had called in recent days.

"Lieutenant Kagan? This is Savanna Robinson. I'm afraid I've found another one. Here at the college, in Scholars' Quad."

While I was calling Kagan, Hamilton called the campus police. Being closer, they showed up first, followed by the city cops about ten minutes later.

That gave me plenty of time to study the body. The boy was wearing a light-colored shirt and darker pants. He lay on his back, limbs akimbo, and a dark stain covered the lower left side of his torso, leading me to think he had either been shot or stabbed. Without turning him over, I couldn't tell.

When Kagan showed up, he simply stood silently staring at the body, then walked all the way around it, never getting closer than about ten feet.

"Okay," he finally said, "who found him?"

"We did," I answered. "We were walking back from the reception."

"And you were the first ones to leave?"

Hamilton answered, "I'm sure we weren't. At first, we thought he was simply passed out drunk. I'm sure anyone else who spotted him might have thought the same."

Kagan nodded, glancing in the direction of the dorms, where loud music and students' voices could still be heard. "That would be more likely, wouldn't it?"

He pulled shoe covers and gloves from his pocket and put them on, then approached the body. Bending down, he picked something up and brought it over to the three of us.

"I hate to jump to conclusions," Kagan said, "but I think this might have something to do with his condition."

It was a knife—an athame—cheaper, lighter, thinner, and narrower than either mine or Agnes's.

Ricard leaned close and aimed the beam of a small flashlight on it. The blade had blood on it.

"He is a bit far from the building to have fallen out of a window, but good luck tracing that," Hamilton said. "That athame is part of the student tool kit they sell in the bookstore. Probably several thousand of them here on campus."

"He could have been playing quidditch and fallen," I said. All three men snorted.

The same woman who had been the medical examiner at Agnes's murder scene walked over and opened a plastic bag. Kagan dropped the knife in it.

"That could do it," the woman said. "Stabbed once in the abdomen, under the ribs. At least that's what I can see right now. No other obvious wounds."

"I think it was safer in Oakland," I said.

"We have had a rash of murders lately," Kagan said. "Do any of you recognize him? I'm going to start with the assumption he was a student."

"Joshua Tupper," Ricard said, "fourth-year student in alchemy."

The name seemed familiar, and I shot him a glance. "Was he one of Kavanaugh's advisees?"

Ricard looked thoughtful for a moment. "You know, I think he was."

Hamilton leaned close to me and quietly said, "It's a small place. Almost everyone has some kind of connection with everyone else."

"And you didn't see anyone else about?" Kagan asked.

"No," I answered. "A couple was walking quite a distance in front of us, but they exited the quad about the time we entered."

"He's been dead for a couple of hours," the woman from the ME's office said, then turned away to go supervise two men who were lifting the body onto a gurney.

"Can we go?" Hamilton asked.

Kagan looked around, then said, "Yes. I know where to find you if I have any more questions."

I walked to my apartment between the two men. We were all very quiet. They dropped me at my door, Hamilton crossed to his, and Ricard continued to the parking lot.

I shut my door, then spent about twenty minutes setting wards on my doors and windows.

CHAPTER 10

On my way to my first class the following morning, I met Emma coming toward me.

"Hi, Dr. Robinson."

"Hello, Emma. Going to the greenhouse?"

"Yes, I just want to check on things. I don't think Lia will make it today, and I don't get out of class until late."

"Is she all right?"

Emma looked around, and seeing no one else was near, said, "I don't know if you heard, but a student was killed on the quad last night. He was Lia's ex-boyfriend."

"Yes, I heard," I said, "but I didn't know him. If there's anything I can do for her, please let me know."

Of course, the buzz in my first class was all about the death, and I could tell the students weren't very attentive. I was also distracted and glad I didn't have to lecture on anything substantial. I handed out the course syllabus, gave them a reading assignment, and talked a little about the history of alchemy.

When I went to lunch at the faculty dining room, I found the conversations around me weren't much different from those in the classroom. Word of the murder had spread, and the rumors weren't always accurate. Just among those I overheard, Joshua Tupper died from a knife, a gunshot, poison, magic, and had fallen from the roof of a building.

It didn't surprise me that people were upset. I was upset too, and I'd never met the boy. I had never felt unsafe on a college campus, but suddenly Wicklow seemed a rather foreboding place.

As I was finishing my lunch, Kelly came in, looked around the room, then rushed over, and sat down at my table.

"I just heard that you were the one who found that student," she said. "How horrible! I didn't even know about it until I showed up for work this morning."

"How late did you stay at the reception?" I asked. The police and crime scene people were still there when I and my professorial escort finally left the quad well past midnight. Of course, she might have stayed the night, but it seemed rather rude to suggest that. We really didn't know each other that well.

"Not long, but the taxi picked me up at Howard Hall, so I didn't leave through the quad. How are you doing?"

"A little shaky," I admitted. "Until last week, I'd never seen a dead person before, except at a funeral, and now it's getting to be a regular occurrence. I think Kagan is starting to wonder about me. At least I have an alibi for both murders."

Kelly laughed a bit nervously. "I don't think murderers usually report their crimes. They're too busy trying to hide their tracks."

I chuckled. "You're an expert?"

"Mystery reader and TV watcher."

"Well, I don't think Kagan watches TV, or he'd know he should be solving the crimes quicker. Most TV detectives take less than an hour."

Kelly shrugged. "If Dr. Phillips has his way, the investigation will evaporate today. He's not happy that the local newspaper picked up on the story. He'd prefer that parents, other than Joshua's of course, never heard about it."

"I can't imagine there is so much interesting news in Wicklow that the media wouldn't pick up a murder story."

"Yeah. Usually, they happen at the Wolf's Den. That's a biker-shifter bar, and the story is on the back page. This one was front page. Anything even slightly scandalous about the college is big news."

"You're saying I should discreetly manage my scandals?"

"Definitely. I'm sure there's a section on that in your tenure evaluation."

In my afternoon lecture, the students were older, and many of them knew the deceased, so it was still the major topic I overheard as I entered the room. I wondered if Kagan was talking to Tupper's classmates, or if Dr. Phillips would even allow it.

It turned out that Charlotte was in my afternoon Intermediate Apothecary Arts class. After the class was over, I saw her huddled with several of her classmates, and their discussion seemed quite animated.

After class, I went back to my rooms, changed clothes, and checked the herb garden and the greenhouse. Two of the undergraduates were working, and they asked me a few questions about fertilizer and watering schedules. They also wanted to chatter at me about the death.

"Did you hear about the murder?" Barbara asked. "They say the body was just lying out in the middle of Scholars' Quad."

"Yes, I heard. I don't think I'll be walking around alone at night," I said.

"Do you think it was a mugging, or something like that, do you?" Charlotte asked. "I talked to someone who knew him, and they said he had a reputation. Poaching on other people's girlfriends."

"Oh? And is that the normal way people handle that here at Wicklow?"

"Huh? No, of course not. But I guess there was a scene last night. At a party." Charlotte stared down at her shoes, then raised her head. "I heard that Lia was part of that."

"Well," I said, "I think there are probably a lot of rumors, most of which have little basis in fact. So far today, I've heard he was killed by every method including little green men with ray guns, so it might be best to do more listening than spreading."

"Yes, ma'am," both girls muttered before going off to attend to their chores.

Emma showed up about twenty minutes later, and I told her about Charlotte's statement.

"I agree with you about the rumors," Emma said. "Everyone has a different theory. But I talked with Lia, and I do know that one has a basis in fact. She was at a party with her boyfriend, and Josh tried to talk with her. The two guys got in a shouting match, and Josh stormed out. I don't think he took their breakup very well."

"So, it was Lia who broke up with him?"

"Yeah. They hooked up when he was a first-year, and she was a year ahead of him. She graduated last spring. At one point, she planned to go to grad school in Boulder, and I know he wasn't happy about that."

"But she ended up staying here?"

"Yeah, but I don't know why." Emma shrugged. "Maybe Corey, her new boyfriend. He's a doctoral student, works as an assistant for Dr. Hamilton. Dr. Kavanaugh offered her this job, which for anyone doing apothecary is kind of a big deal."

"It sounds like she has a lot of drama going on," I said. "So, she didn't work here last year?"

Emma laughed. "She started work here after mid-winter break. She does like men. I don't know, she always seems to be looking for something better, and Josh was the jealous type. Her father has been married a bunch of times, and so has her mother. She grew up splitting time between them, and also spent time at a boarding school in Switzerland. I just don't think she's very happy."

"How did she and Agnes get along?"

"About like everyone and Agnes got along. Dr. Robinson, Agnes was prickly, you know? Very private, and particular. She had her own way of doing things, and she was very judgmental. But she really was a nice person. She could have a sharp tongue, but she wasn't ever mean. If someone didn't do things the way she thought they ought to be done, she'd grumble, but she'd fix it. She could have reported some of the girls for a number of things, but she never did."

"But she argued with Dr. Kavanaugh."

"Oh, yeah. He thought she should automatically defer to him on everything because he had a PhD. And, you know, she was a woman. But she really did know more about growing plants than he did."

"Who is Mrs. Donnelly?" I asked.

"Helen? She was the greenhouse and garden manager. We all worked for her, and she reported to Dr. Kavanaugh. She fought with him like cats and dogs." A sly grin passed across Emma's face. "I think they might have been lovers, not recently, but long ago. You know how you get that vibe from people sometimes? His death hit her hard, and when the college posted the opening to fill his position, she turned in her resignation. Rumor is that she bought an old nursery on the north side of town, and she was going to start a business with Agnes."

CHAPTER 13

Kelly stopped by with a bottle of wine after she got off work.

"Where do you get the booze?" I asked. "Surely you don't take it to work with you."

She chuckled. "You can buy it from the bartender in the Faculty Club. The selection's limited, and it costs a little more than from a liquor store in town, but everybody does it. Some professors order wine by the case."

I grabbed a couple of wine glasses from the kitchen, along with a corkscrew, and we sat down in front of the fireplace.

"Is everyone still panicking about Joshua Tupper?" I asked. "In my classes today, getting the students' attention was a real chore."

"Oh, yeah. I stopped by and saw Katy on my way over here, and she said the calls from parents and the press have been non-stop all day."

"I'm sure. They send Billy and Susie here and expect we'll protect them from all of life's possible misfortunes. And if we don't protect them from themselves, we're terrible people."

"I guess that's natural. I expect to feel safe here. Until Brett was killed, I always did."

I nodded. "I was pretty shaky when I got home last night. I went around and checked all the windows and doors, then renewed the wards. But once I got in bed and my mind sort of relaxed, I realized that Kavanaugh, Agnes and probably our young Mr. Tupper, all knew whoever killed them, and weren't afraid."

Kelly poured the wine and held up her glass. After I clinked mine against it, she said, "Katy told me Kagan said that Joshua's wallet and keys were missing. When they went to his room, it looked as though it had been searched and his laptop is missing."

Shaking my head, I said, "In every case, it looks like the killer wanted something."

"Have you taken a look at the books in that box we found at Brett's?"

"Nope, haven't even opened the safe. Did you talk to your mom?"

"Yeah, I did. She says there is a notation in Uncle Harold's ledger book about a GG that he purchased for five thousand pounds. Other than that, nothing. They haven't found anything she can tie to those initials, and it doesn't appear that he sold it. Or maybe he paid money to someone with the initials GG."

"When did he buy it?"

"About a year ago."

"So, just before the letters started between him and Kavanaugh."

Kelly nodded.

"A lot of money," I said, and Kelly nodded again. "Want to take a look? I'm curious what's under those two books on top."

"Sure."

We took the garden entrance to my laboratory, locked the door behind us, and I opened the alchemy safe. Kavanaugh's box sat there, as malevolent or harmless as ever, depending on how one looked at it. I took it out and set it on a workbench.

"Should we draw a circle?" I asked.

"I don't think that will be necessary," Kelly said. "I don't plan on opening that one book, let alone reading it aloud."

"Agreed."

I drew on a pair of surgical gloves and lifted out the book Hamilton had identified as Kavanaugh's grimoire. I set it on the bench and opened it. On the third page a list of names started with a date in 1432. Three pages later, the last name on the list was Brett Kavanaugh, August 8, 1978.

"And no one seems to know anything about his family," I said. I paged through the book. The early entries were in Gaelic, then some in archaic English were sprinkled in with entries in Gaelic, then around the beginning of the seventeenth century, everything was written in Latin.

I reached into the box and pulled out the book that had been under the grimoire. "Recognize this one?"

"Looks like a copy of one of Da Vinci's notebooks," Kelly said. She took it and leafed through it. "Maybe a couple of hundred years old, but not worth a lot. The British Museum has digitized all the ones they can get their hands on. One of the originals sold for thirty million a few years ago, but I doubt this would bring more than a couple of thousand. However, it is interesting that this is the one dealing with poisons."

I took it back from her and sifted through it. "Nothing a good alchemist or apothecary wouldn't know already. The techniques are severely dated."

"What's under the nasty book?" Kelly asked.

Setting the two books we had already looked at aside, I slid the *Maleficium Spiritus* into the box's empty space. I looked at the book that had been hidden, and laughed.

"I know this is a copy—a mass production copy—although

why Kavanaugh would even want it, let alone put it somewhere safe, is a mystery."

Kelly leaned over to look at it. "The Alchemist's Handbook?"

"Yes, written by a charlatan in the twentieth century. I've assigned it to my grad students in Cavecolito for a history of alchemy class, but it has very little practical use. I don't even think the author was a witch."

Kelly sighed. "Maybe, but Brett thought enough of these to hide them behind some pretty good spells. The *Maleficium* and his grimoire I can understand, but why the others? If he was a collector, he surely would know their value."

"And the book we're looking for, GG, isn't here. If anyone was going to commit murder for a book, the *Maleficium* would be it."

"Yeah, and it would even show you how to do it."

I snorted. "Four murders, and only one of them might remotely be tied to witchcraft."

Kelly shook her head. "Someone tried to kill Agnes with witchcraft."

"And didn't get the job done. Agnes might have been stronger than her attacker. I wonder if Kagan checked with hospitals and doctors to see if anyone sought treatment that day."

My lecture classes were scheduled for Tuesdays and Thursdays, and I scheduled my tutorials on Mondays and Wednesdays in the late afternoon. A dozen of students coming into my home felt rather invasive, so I made sure everything I cared about was put away, and the door to my bedroom was closed.

The Wednesday group were apothecary students, fourth

year and graduates, including Emma and Ophelia. I fixed tea and set out two plates of cookies.

In addition to the two girls who worked in the greenhouse, the students included two more girls and two boys. All the students but one were graduates, working on advanced degrees in Apothecary Arts. One girl was a fourth-year student, due to graduate before Christmas and already accepted to a graduate program.

"I'm not sure how your other professors run their tutorials," I said when everyone had found a place to sit and had their tea and snacks. "What I prefer to do is let you decide what we discuss. Each week, one of you will propose a topic you're interested in. Consider nothing out of bounds, but please keep it in the realm of apothecary. Now, for this week, does anyone have a question that has been driving you crazy?"

The students glanced around at each other, all of them showing some uneasiness. Finally, one of the young men spoke.

"I read somewhere that necromancy is a form of alchemy. Is that true?"

I fought to suppress a smile. "Yes, and you're all aware that necromantic spells are completely off limits here at Wicklow, right?"

After everyone enthusiastically agreed that necromancy was against the rules, I continued.

"Okay. This comes under the heading of just because you know how to do something doesn't mean you should do it. And in this particular case, I can tell you that it's something you don't want to do. Yes, I can cast a spell that will animate your dead rabbit or old Uncle Jake. And then what do you do with them? They'll do what you tell them to, but only as long as you're physically there directing them. Your zombie has no brain. You can't program them like a computer and turn them loose to do your bidding. Do you understand what I'm saying?"

Emma leaned closer. "What about a golem?"

"You know this is more a topic for an alchemy course than an apothecary course, right? But for today, we'll stray a little off topic. Golems are part of the Kabbalah's study of alchemy. And I'll let an expert in that field address it. I have studied how they're made, and they are different from what is normally considered necromancy. A golem is like a puppet, and they can be animated and directed at a distance. Now, I know that several hundred years ago a coven in Germany conducted experiments that involved summoning demons and using them to reanimate corpses. A couple of those witches were burned at the stake by Church authorities, and the rest were beheaded by other witches. Not exactly a happy ending."

It took some time, but I was able to steer the conversation around to questions concerning the Apothecary Arts. When the session was over, I ushered everyone out the door and stood with my back against it, relieved that once again I had survived a close encounter with a group of brilliant students. Deciding that a celebration was in order, I set to figuring out what I should do with the rest of my evening.

CHAPTER 14

My first decision was that I didn't want to cook, so I grabbed my purse and headed toward the Faculty Club. The closeness of the restaurant made it very tempting. As I locked my door, I heard a noise behind me and turned to see David Hamilton coming out of the door leading to his apartment.

"Going out someplace?" he asked as he strolled toward me.

"Dinner." I motioned in the direction of the faculty dining room. "I don't feel like cooking."

He chuckled. "Considering *my* cooking skills, the chef at the club is always far preferable, and the costs aren't much more. Mind some company?"

"Not at all. I don't know about you," I said, "but I think a lot of the women on this campus feel far more afraid than they did a week ago."

"I think a lot fewer instructors invite pretty coeds to their rooms than they did before Brett was killed," Hamilton responded. He chuckled at the look I shot him.

"Oh, not me. I don't invite students to my rooms. I'm a bit

too private for that. I hold my tutorials at the library." He winked. "Fewer fireplace pokers."

We walked through the campus and past the place where we had found Joshua Tupper two nights before. In the faculty dining room, we were shown to a table by the window overlooking the quad.

"Have you always been a bachelor?"

He grinned. "That's a novel way of asking the question. Yes, as a matter of fact. Never been married or owned a house. Some might say that I graduated but never grew up."

"But you do own a car?"

"Yes, but I don't drive it very much."

"Let me guess. Dr. Kavanaugh drove a Jaguar, Dr. Ricard drives a Porsche, but I'd say you were more for a BMW or Mercedes."

"A Toyota SUV. It's more practical, especially during Pennsylvania winters, and I like to camp and fish. You don't have a car, do you?"

I shook my head. "In San Francisco, renting a parking place usually cost more than a car payment. I learned to make do with a bicycle. I've ordered one, but it will be two or three weeks before it arrives."

"With all those hills?"

I shook my head. "Cycling is good for you, but I tried to avoid the hilly part of town. I was in Oakland, near Berkeley. I took BART and the bus to Sausalito when I taught there."

The waiter came and took our orders. I noted that David ordered the special, as did Ricard the night I dined with him.

"So, you eat here often?" I asked.

"About half my meals. It also cuts down on all that grocery shopping."

I could certainly agree on that.

"I noticed that there seems to be some distance between you and Dr. Ricard," I said.

"In a small community, old differences don't always heal," Hamilton said. "There's a group of us who all came here around the same time. Brett, Anton, and me, along with Jerome and Edmund. We're about the same age, and we all started teaching here within a few years of each other."

"Jerome and Edmund?"

"Jerome Carver and Edmund Phillips. Jerome is the only one who has married. Once, we were all very close. Time and different interests, and we sort of drifted apart."

"I heard a rumor that several of you were in love with the same woman."

Hamilton rolled his eyes. "I heard that rumor, also."

When he showed no interest in following that line of conversation, I dropped it. If I wanted to find out more, Katy always seemed ready to gossip.

On the way back to our apartments, we saw Lia and a tall young man walk out of the breezeway between the faculty apartments, turn right, and go into the west building of Howard Quad.

"That's a residential building, right?" I asked.

"Graduate student dorm," David said. "That building across the way, also. And the one behind us is for single junior faculty and post-docs."

"So, that building they went into is right next to my building, and right next to Brett Kavanaugh's apartment."

"Yes, that's right, why?"

"Just trying to orient myself. I'm new, remember?"

He chuckled. "Oh, I noticed."

"Wondering if any of the students heard anything the night he was killed."

"You're assuming any of them were home studying instead of drinking in the pub."

"Right. Silly me. You know, I love to cook, but it's a pain to cook for one person. Would a bottle of wine be too much to exchange for a home-cooked meal occasionally?"

He cocked his head a bit to the side and gave me a silly grin. "I think that's a brilliant idea. Let me know when."

Kelly offered to take me to the grocery store on Saturday. While looking for a parking place, we drove by Back to Basics, and I noticed the front door was open. Curious, we walked by the shop.

Inside, we saw the furniture had been put back in place, the goods spilled across the floor had been picked up, and a woman with light-brown hair, in blue jeans and a t-shirt, was in the process of sweeping the floor. No trace of the blood pool remained.

I stuck my head through the doorway and said, "Hi."

"Hello," the woman responded. "We aren't open as yet, but I hope to have a grand re-opening next week."

"We'll try to stop by," I said. "Did you buy the shop?"

"Oh, no, it belonged to my sister. Did you know Agnes?"

"We work at the college. Actually, we're the ones who found her. I'm Savanna Robinson and this is Kelly Grace. I'm so sorry for your loss."

The woman walked over and extended her hand.

"Iris Bishop. It was such a shock. The police don't seem to have a clue."

"It's their standard mode of operation," Kelly said. "Luckily, there isn't much crime here, because they aren't very good at solving the ones that do occur."

"So, you're going to operate the shop?" I asked.

"Yes, I think so. Agnes had an agreement with a woman who operates a greenhouse here, and they planned on expanding the offerings. I met with her yesterday, and it seems like a great opportunity. I really didn't have anything holding me in Salem, so it's a chance to try something new."

"Are you an herbalist?"

Iris smiled. "Botanist, herbalist, apothecary. I guess you know Helen Donnelly. She said that she also taught at the college."

"I know her," Kelly said. "Savanna just started this term."

Iris turned and looked around the shop. "I have a lot of work to do in a week. I'm going to display the herbs and botanicals differently, as well as doing bulk sales. We won't have a full inventory at first, but as soon as production at the nursery ramps up, I hope to supply all the witches in the area with fresh ingredients."

"And all the cooks, I hope," Kelly said with a smile.

"Oh, definitely. And the grocery stores. I have a meeting with the manager of the one over there on Monday."

As we resumed our trek to the store, I said, "David told me that this is a small place, and everyone is sort of intertwined."

"That's the truth."

"But, you know, other than Katy, I haven't talked to anyone who really liked Brett Kavanaugh. Even she didn't seem to approve of his relations with women."

"And you know something?" Kelly said. "He really didn't give a damn. Pompous, arrogant, condescending son of a…"

"Yes, those are the words almost everyone uses to describe him."

CHAPTER 15

I answered a knock on my door to find Lieutenant Kagan standing there.

"Oh. It's you," I said. "How can I help the police today?"

"I'm sorry. I take it you expected someone else. I'd like to talk to you about one of your employees."

"A friend called from Pittsburgh and is coming here. I'm afraid you're misinformed, though. I don't have any employees. Perhaps you mean one of my students?"

"Perhaps. May I come in?"

I stood aside and allowed him to enter, then closed the door, and locked it.

"May I get you something to drink? Some tea or lemonade?" I asked.

"No, thank you. This is just a courtesy call. Are you aware that one of your students, Ophelia Harkness, was involved with Joshua Tupper, the young man who was killed in Scholars' Quad?" Rather than sit down, he stood, nervously shifting his weight from one foot to the other, and staring at a small notebook in his hand.

"I was told that he was her ex-boyfriend."

Kagan nodded. "Evidently, there was a row earlier that night at a party in one of the dormitories. She accused him of stalking her, and then Tupper and her now boyfriend, another student named Corey Lindsay, got into a physical altercation. At the end of which, Lindsay yelled, 'Come near her again and I'll kill you.'"

"Oh, dear." I decided that I wanted to sit down—whether Kagan did or not—so I took a seat on the couch. "You know how it is at that age, Lieutenant. Everything is so dramatic."

"Yes, and if young Mr. Tupper hadn't ended up dead, no one would be asking questions about it."

"Well, I don't think I can help you, Lieutenant. I haven't spoken to Ophelia since this all happened. I was told she doesn't feel well."

There was a knock on the door, and I jumped up. "That's probably Steve. Excuse me."

I went to the door, and came back with a tall young man carrying a suitcase.

"Steve, this is Lieutenant Kagan, with the local police. Lieutenant, this is my friend Steven McCallum, from San Francisco."

"Oh, well, I guess I'll be running along," Kagan said. "Do you know if Ms. Harkness is working in the greenhouse this afternoon?"

I shook my head. "No, I don't. But if not, you might try her dorm room."

I showed the detective out, and when I came back, Steve was sprawled on the couch. A little over six-feet tall, with a slender, athletic build, thick light-brown hair, Steven McCallum was every girl's dream—and every gay man's, which was more important to Steve. He worked as a model and an occasional actor in California.

"Can I hit you up for something to drink?" he asked.

"Sure, lemonade, water, wine? Or maybe a cup of tea?"

"Lemonade sounds great. Have you been a bad girl? What's the fat cop want? Or is he an admirer?"

I poured him a glass, and one for myself, then sat down and gave him a quick overview of my introduction to Wicklow.

"Lovely," he said when I finished. "And you thought it would be a good idea if I came here to share all this fun with you?"

I winked. "I'd hate to be accused of selfishness."

He made a point of looking around the room. "Nice digs. Is everything here so nineteenth century?"

"Pretty much, but they have paved the streets in town, replaced the water troughs with parking meters, and I'm told most places have running water, indoor toilets, and electricity. Electricity was a retrofit here. I haven't checked the plumbing very closely, but it works better than at my apartment in Oakland. When's your first interview?"

"Ten o'clock tomorrow. They put me up at the Wayfarer's Inn in the city. Do you know where that is?"

"Not really. Let me call someone." I called Kelly. "Hi, a friend of mine is in town for an interview. Where is the Wayfarer's Inn?"

It turned out it was next to the grocery store. Kelly offered to take him there, and stopped by later when she got off work. As I expected, her eyes lit up when she saw Steven.

"Well, hello! Kelly Grace, at your service."

"Hi, Steven McCallum," he replied. Knowing him well, I could see the hesitation and reticence in his manner. Steven was used to women throwing themselves at him, and to their varied reactions when he wasn't receptive.

The three of us and Steven's bag piled into Kelly's car, and she drove to the hotel.

"This is where the college puts everyone from out of town," Kelly told us. "Savanna, if you were here for a conference, this is probably where you stayed."

"Maybe. I really don't remember, except that it was a little too far to walk, and the bus took forever to show up."

Kelly nodded. "About two miles. And the buses here always take forever to show up."

"How's the food?" Steven asked. He waved a piece of paper. "This is a voucher I can use either at the hotel or at the Faculty Club. I guess that's a dining room on campus."

"Decent breakfast at the inn," Kelly said. "Diner quality. But I'd rather eat on campus for lunch and dinner."

"Well, I'm starving," Steven said. "Let me check in, and perhaps you ladies would join me for dinner?"

While Kelly and I waited in the car, I said, "This is really nice of you. You'll bring him back after dinner?"

"It's on my way home. You didn't tell me that this guy looks like a Greek god."

"Add another 'g' to that description," I said with a laugh.

"You're kidding."

"Nope. That's one of the reasons he and I get along so well. He makes a great wing man because we have very different tastes in men."

Kelly sighed. "There are downsides to being a single woman in Wicklow."

"Lack of single men? I haven't had time to really investigate, but all of those I've met seem to be confirmed bachelors."

"Almost all of the men you've met are employed by the college. Not a very representative sample, since they can read, write, count past ten, and know the difference between a napkin and their sleeve. And yes, very confirmed bachelors."

"I met Lieutenant Kagan."

"A typical local male."

"He's a little young for me," I said.

"I wish I could say that. I kept giving him lame excuses until he finally stopped asking me out."

Savanna laughed. "How long did that take?"

Kelly shook her head. "A couple of years. He is incredibly persistent."

"I wish I could say that about his detective work."

About that time, Steve came out of the inn and slid into the front seat of the car. Kelly drove to the college, parked next to the library, and the three of us walked to the Faculty Club.

"My, this is nice," Steve said, looking around before opening his menu.

"And the food reflects the atmosphere," I said. "Especially nice since they run it as a break-even enterprise. Much cheaper than the other high-end restaurants in town."

During dinner, I mainly listened as Kelly chattered on about the college and the town, their history, and answered questions Steve had. A lot of it was almost verbatim what she'd told me a couple of weeks before.

Immediately after the waiter cleared our dishes, David Hamilton stopped by our table. I made introductions, then David leaned down to me.

"Kagan arrested Corey Lindsay this afternoon."

"For Tupper's death?"

David nodded. "Evidently he also questioned him about Brett's murder. Corey's father contacted me, and I helped arrange for a local lawyer—a fishing buddy of mine. He told me that Kagan thinks Ophelia Harkness had a relationship with Brett."

"Oh, how interesting. Has the lawyer spoken with Ophelia?"

Hamilton shook his head. "Can't get near her. She's also engaged a lawyer."

CHAPTER 16

When I came home from class the following day, I found Steve sitting on my front stoop. He looked very professional in a gray suit—the same suit he'd worn to defend his dissertation. I wondered how many suits he had. Academia in the Bay Area wasn't terribly formal.

"How did it go?" I asked.

His face lit up with a smile. "Nailed it. Decent salary, and a free place to live. Not as fancy as your place, but nice enough." He gestured in the direction of Howard Quad, and I assumed he had been offered one of the studio apartments set aside for junior faculty, or sometimes senior graduate students.

"Congratulations! Come on in and I'll pour you a drink. When do you start?"

"A week from Monday. Now, all I have to do is figure out how to get my stuff here from California."

"Work on your teleportation spell."

He barked a laugh. "You know, I've been working on that one since I was eight years old, and still don't have the hang of it."

"Me neither. I'll give you the information on the shipping company I used."

"Thanks, I'll take it. But the big problem is my car. I can't drive here from San Francisco in a weekend."

"Ask for some time off, or wait until the first break. I think there's a week surrounding Samhain. Did you meet the ladies who'll be working for you?"

I dumped my briefcase and the books I'd been carrying on my desk, and went into the kitchen to retrieve a bottle of wine and a pair of glasses.

"I met a couple of them. Two graduate students named Emma and Ophelia, and a younger girl, Charlotte. The setup here is nice, and the greenhouse is quite state of the art."

"Plus some. You and Emma need to recast the wards. We evidently do get occasional violent storms in this area, so you need to protect the glass. I'll have a list of botanicals I need for my classes by Monday. I'm sure other professors will have their own lists."

Steve nodded, loosened his tie, took a sip of his wine, and leaned back in his chair. "Thanks. Is Doctor Carver as humorless as he seems?"

"Not completely, but as Kelly describes him, he's not a people person. On the other hand, I wouldn't expect him to micromanage. I almost never see him. You'll probably deal with Katy, his secretary."

He chuckled. "He doesn't strike me as having much of a personality at all."

"It is one of his charms. But he seems to wear what few emotions he has on his sleeve. I take it that he was relieved you agreed to take the job?"

"You're right about showing his emotions. I'd love to play poker with him. I didn't expect that he'd throw in a free place to live."

"My understanding is that there aren't a lot of rentals in this area. Students are required to live on campus their first three years, and there are these apartments for single faculty. I'm not sure I'd want to share this space with someone. How was Ophelia doing when you saw her?"

"Okay. Quiet. She didn't say much."

I raised an eyebrow. "She's the extrovert, she and Charlotte. Boy crazy, so I'm a little surprised you didn't get a rise out of her."

"From what you told me last night, that hasn't been going too well for her lately."

"No, it hasn't. I'm not sure if she has poor taste in men, or she just attracts the wrong sort."

"Any idea where the gay crowd hangs out here in Wicklow?"

"Nope. It wasn't on my priority list. The town isn't very large, though, so I don't think it should take an extended search to find out. There's always Pittsburgh on weekends."

"I think I owe you dinner," he said. "Change into something more comfortable, and let's go paint the town."

"Thanks. I'll show you a place I like." I glanced at my watch. "I'd better get a move on. The bus will be here in twenty minutes, and as Kelly said, it's a bit of a hike into town from here."

The location of my apartment shielded me from most of the noise from the dormitories and the student pub. There was also a small pub that was off limits to undergrads—on the ground floor of the junior faculty housing building between the two quads. Faculty, staff, and grad students only.

But at about eleven o'clock that night, I heard some strange noises through the front door. I waited for a minute, then the noise ceased, and I didn't think any more about it.

The following morning, knowing I couldn't put it off any longer, I gathered the material I needed to have copied for students. My assigned classes were Introduction to Alchemy, first semester Intermediate Apothecary Arts, and a senior seminar in Advanced Alchemy. In addition, I had two graduate tutorials—five students in Alchemy, and six students for Apothecary Arts.

The Intro to Alchemy course had an enormous number of students, but I had taught it so often at other colleges that I could have probably done it in my sleep. I would lecture twice a week in the largest room in the college—the theater auditorium in the President's house. But I had ten grad students assigned to do the grading and hold the tutorials. The other courses were capped at twelve students each. Carver provided two senior undergraduate assistants to help with my grading, typing, copying, and other chores in those courses.

I gritted my teeth when he told me all of this, reminding myself of what they were paying and his promise to hire more professors. The position announcements had already been posted, so I hoped they filled them before I had to do all of that the next year.

With a briefcase full of paper, my purse, and an umbrella that I decided to take due to the dark clouds that had moved in overnight, I was juggling things when I opened the door. As a result, I dropped the umbrella. Nudging the door open with the briefcase, I bent down to pick up the umbrella. Then my purse slipped off my shoulder.

Mumbling curses, I set the briefcase down and pushed it through the door with my foot. There was a loud noise, and the door slammed into me. The stout oak door protected me from the full force of the explosion, knocking me down behind it. I lay there, curled into a ball, stunned. Something hurt. Maybe a few somethings.

My ears were ringing, but I could hear hurried footsteps

coming nearer from the far end of the breezeway. The door was pushed, squeezing me, and I cried out. I sensed someone standing over me.

"Dr. Robinson? Savanna? Are you all right?" David Hamilton asked, a frantic note in his voice. His looming presence shrank as he crouched down beside me and put his hand on my arm. "Savanna?"

I tried to find my voice, tried to sit up. Things just weren't working properly. The effort was too great. Managing to lift my arm, I reached out to him. He put his hand on my arm, his other hand under it, and pulled me into a sitting position.

"Are you all right? Are you injured?"

"I don't know." I could barely hear myself.

Excited voices beyond the door. Someone tried to push it open.

"Carefully!" Hamilton shouted.

A forehead and a pair of eyes peeked around the edge of the door.

"Get a doctor," Hamilton ordered. The eyes disappeared, to be replaced by a different pair.

I managed to focus on his face. "I don't think I'm hurt very badly," I said. "But I am terribly twisted and uncomfortable. Do you think you can help me stand?"

He stood, braced his back against the door, and reached down, putting his hands in my armpits. Straightening, he pulled me up, and I managed to untangle my legs and lean back against the wall.

I took a deep breath, and said, "Perhaps a chair."

He guided me into the sitting room and gently pushed me down into the nearest chair. I watched as he scanned me, looking for injuries. Evidently deciding I wasn't in imminent danger of death, he went to the kitchen and returned with a glass of water, which he handed me.

And then a woman wearing a white coat appeared, picking

up my wrist to check my pulse, peering into my eyes, and then laying one hand on my head, the other on my leg.

"You are one lucky girl," the woman said after a minute. "When I saw the damage outside, my heart about stopped."

"The door protected me. I didn't ever step outside," I said.

"Well, I still want to take you to the infirmary for observation. I'm Dr. Evans, by the way."

Evans was about my age, with short brown hair and the sort of kindly face one would hope a healer would have.

"Fine with me, as long as you don't expect me to walk. I'm still feeling a bit shaky."

"No problem," Evans said. "I have a couple of orderlies and a witch taxi waiting for you.

After they loaded me on a gurney, and the orderlies used magic to float it over the stoop and down the steps to the quad, I understood what a witch taxi was. Hamilton was still there, walking by my side and looking worried.

"My briefcase?" I asked.

"I think you'll need a new one," he answered.

"The papers inside?"

"Mostly intact, but some are the worse for wear."

"I was taking them for Kelly to copy, then I was going to give them to Kagan."

"Ah, I wondered. I took a look at a couple. I can take care of all that for you."

They floated me up the stairs into the infirmary on the ground floor of the Admin Building, and into a room where two nurses took my clothes, dressed me in a hospital gown, and put me to bed.

Dr. Evans and another doctor came, examined me, then left, leaving one nurse to watch over me. I had just woken up, and had three cups of tea with my breakfast, so I shouldn't have been sleepy, but I dozed off anyway. My last conscious thought was, *Why would someone want to kill me?*

Soft whispers woke me. Opening my eyes, I saw David Hamilton and a nurse standing near the door of my room.

"What time is it?" I asked.

"You slept for about an hour," the nurse answered.

David walked over and put a stack of paper held together with a large clip on the nightstand. "Kelly has your copies." His eyes flicked toward the door. "The cops are here."

"Did you see anything?" I asked.

He shook his head. "I was at the end of the breezeway, on my way to my office, when I heard the explosion. I turned around and saw the smoke coming from your door."

"No one else around?"

"When I got there, I saw a couple of people coming from the parking lot. Otherwise, no. I've already talked to the police. Do you feel up to it?"

"Yes, I'm fine. I think the adrenaline and shock have worn off. I really wasn't hurt, was I?"

"The doctor said we need to watch for concussion symptoms."

He turned and nodded to the nurse, who opened the door. An older man in a police uniform came in, followed by Sam Kagan.

"Dr. Robinson?" the uniformed man asked. "I'm Alistair Crumley, chief of the campus police department. Do you feel up to answering some questions?"

I tried to give him a smile. "I think I have more questions than answers, but I'm glad to tell you what I know." I went on to tell them what happened from my point of view.

"So, you didn't see anyone?"

"I never made it through the door. The first person I saw was Dr. Hamilton."

Kagan walked over and looked at the papers on the table, then looked at me.

"Those are for you," I said. "I found them mixed in with some scholarly papers in Dr. Kavanaugh's desk. I planned to call you after I got to my office."

He picked them up and thumbed through them, then tucked them under his arm.

"Thanks. Any idea why someone tried to kill you?"

"The only thing that comes to mind is someone might have seen me go with you to Kavanaugh's apartment. And you've come to my place a couple of times. I don't care what anyone else thinks, this and his death have to be connected."

That caused Kagan's eyebrows to shoot up, but that was his only reaction.

"She has asked quite a few questions of various people about Dr. Kavanaugh and his murder," Hamilton said, "but I think you would agree that's understandable, in her situation."

"What if he was killed because someone didn't like alchemists?" I asked. "Or they don't want this position filled? I've been here less than a month, and I never heard of him before."

"Or they don't like blonds," Hamilton said. Everyone looked at him, and he shrugged. "Both she and Brett are blond. Or, in his case, was."

"We are persecuted a lot," I said, and gave him a wink. "People are jealous because we have more fun."

Both Kagan and Crumley rolled their eyes.

"I also discovered Agnes Bishop and Joshua Tupper. Maybe someone thinks I know more than I do about their murders."

After the police left, I asked David, "What about the other folder in my briefcase? The one that had classroom stuff?"

"I gave it to Katy. It didn't look like something Kagan would be interested in."

"Well, I guess I should stop lying around and get some work done. Nurse? May I have my clothes, please?"

"Let me know before you go back to your place," David said. "I set a ward at the end of the hall to block your apartment. You don't have a door, and I didn't think you would appreciate strangers wandering around in there, whether they were in uniform or not."

That was a surprise, but a pleasant one. "Thank you," I said. "One would think the police would keep whoever planted the bomb out, but we've seen that their procedures in securing crime scenes are rather unprofessional."

The nurse called the doctor, who came and examined me again, then pronounced me well and let me go.

CHAPTER 17

When I left my office that afternoon, I found David, Kelly, and Kagan waiting for me.

"Are you my guard detail?"

Kagan looked sheepish, Kelly laughed, and David simply dipped his head.

"I would like to talk with you about the bomb," Kagan said. "At your place."

"As long as you're buying the drinks, I'm at your disposal," I responded, and enjoyed his spluttering reply that he was on duty.

As we walked across the quad, I said, "So, only a few days after I first walked into a classroom, and I'm already the talk of the campus. I assume some of the students here have friends in San Francisco and heard what kind of witch with a b I really am."

Again, Kelly chuckled. Too bad that I couldn't find a man who thought I was that funny, but David's mouth showed a bit of a smirk as he flicked me a glance from the corner of his eye. I always seemed to intimidate most men, either with my intelligence or my power. I'd also been called cold, but I wasn't sure how to fix any of it.

When we reached my home, the reality of the blast's power hit home. The shredded remains of my briefcase sat twenty feet away from the door. The door itself was splintered and buckled; the door frame torn loose from the wall. That was probably the only reason the door still hung on its hinges. The three-inch thick oak door was at least one hundred fifty years old, almost as hard as iron, but it would have to be replaced.

"This was one serious bomb," Kagan said as they examined the damage. "We haven't figured out how it was set off. No evidence of a detonator or trip wire. Maybe triggered remotely?"

Picking my way carefully through the debris, I ran my hands over the door, the frame, and the sill.

"Nitroglycerine," I announced. "Probably set off by a spell. When I pushed my briefcase through the doorway, the spell that held the vial against the door frame let it drop."

I walked away in a straight line from the small crater in the stone by the door. Thirty feet along, I found what I was looking for. I bent down and picked it up, then walked back to the group, holding up a small piece of black rubber.

"Your forensics people might find remnants of a glass test tube scattered about," I said. "This was the stopper. I'd check the top of it to see if there is a thumb print, but I doubt it. I would wear gloves working with this stuff."

"Nitro?" Kagan asked. "How can you tell?"

"I'm an alchemist. I can detect the residue. I show students how to make it—and why they shouldn't. Simple stuff. Glycerol, nitric acid, and sulfuric acid—all of which are present in every chemistry lab on campus. Really touchy, so you bottle it, freeze it to move it, attach it to the doorframe, and it thaws out hanging there. That makes it even more touchy."

"And you show students how to make it?" Kagan seemed appalled.

"They can get the recipe and the steps online," I said. "The way I show it to them, I make a tiny amount from a distance of about fifty feet out in a pasture, or someplace like that, using levitation rather than my hands. When it's finished, I let it cool a little while I lecture them on how dangerous it is, then shake the test tube, and blow up the table and everything I used to make it."

Hamilton burst out in a loud guffaw while Kelly chuckled. After a moment, Kagan allowed himself a chuckle as well.

"Hey," I said, "a lot of these kids are fearless. They think they're invincible. Unless you can cast a substantial personal shield, and still maintain dexterity, I wouldn't touch that stuff. I need them to know there are some things you don't do, even if you know how."

"Like summoning a demon," Kelly said.

"Exactly."

David turned to Kagan. "How long is this going to remain a crime scene? Until the college can repair the door, she can't stay there. Five or six months, like Brett's place?"

Kagan turned bright red. "Not tonight, but I'll try to finish here tomorrow."

"I have a spare room," Kelly said. "Go get an overnight bag and clothes for the weekend."

I knew David didn't have a spare room, but I caught myself hoping—just a little bit—that he might offer me a place. I probably would decline it, but the idea was kind of exciting.

I looked to Hamilton, who nodded. Kagan was turned away from him, and I saw David sketch a rune and speak a word. With that, I picked my way through the ruins of my doorway, and went in to pack. Remembering Kavanaugh's apartment, I also cleaned out the perishables from the refrigerator.

Kelly lived in a small two-bedroom bungalow three blocks east of Main Street, and a mile north of the college. White, with blue trim, a white picket fence, flowers, a patch of grass in the front, and a vegetable garden in the back. Inside, it looked more like an exotic foreign bazaar, with rugs, figurines, and wall hangings from all over the world.

"Some of this stuff I collected on holiday, some my mum or aunt brought me. I'll be doing London again at Christmas, but I'm thinking of the Mediterranean for spring break."

She took me to a quiet little German restaurant owned by the descendants of witches fleeing persecution in Europe during the late seventeenth century. They immigrated to Pennsylvania, the colony of religious freedom. Construction workers needed to be fed, and so they came to Wicklow and started their restaurant when John Howard started building his college.

Afterward, we went back to Kelly's, and I went to the kitchen to brew some chamomile tea. While I waited for the water to boil, a small bookshelf in the corner caught my attention. Thirteen cookbooks and a couple of 'household tips' books by a popular television cook—From the Kitchen Witch's Kitchen—lined the shelf.

"I have a couple of those," I said to Kelly. "You must really like them. That's the whole collection, isn't it?"

Kelly laughed. "And I've tried every one of those recipes. Mum wants them to be idiotproof before she puts them in a book, and I've always been the designated idiot."

"Loretta Grace is your mother?"

"Yup. That's where the money came from for me to attend Wicklow. Da is a civil servant. A British diplomat in Washington doesn't get paid well enough to afford this place."

We discussed the bomb, the students she had caught trying

to enter a restricted area of the museum, and the three murders.

"I've decided someone has it out for apothecaries," I said. "Kavanaugh, Agnes, now me. Tupper was studying alchemy. Someone must have sold a bad potion to the killer's grandmother or something."

"Giving up on the Gambler Grimoire theory?"

I shrugged. "You told me Joshua Tupper's room was searched and his computer is missing. Grimoires and computers are missing for all the victims. I assume the cops searched Corey Lindsay's room when they arrested him. Since they haven't charged him with three murders, I also assume they didn't find Agnes's or Kavanaugh's computers."

"Or grimoires," Kelly said. "Those are also identifiable." She shook her head. "There are places in town where you could pawn a grimoire, but I doubt any of the dealers would be willing to touch items associated with a recent murder victim. The cops did ask me to verify Ophelia's and Corey's computers. Their registrations checked out."

"Where could a student hide things like that?"

"Other than their room? Maybe where they work, if they have a job. I can imagine a lot of places I could hide a book in the library."

I laughed. "You mean, just about any shelf? But maybe I should check out the greenhouse and the laboratories. Places where Ophelia has access."

"You know, Tupper's murder feels different than the others," Kelly said. "A professor or a staff member would have a lot more places to hide the loot—especially if he or she lives off campus."

The kettle whistled, and Kelly poured hot water into my cup.

"I've noticed that you use a lot of Latin," Kelly said. "We don't even know what language the mythical Gambler Grimoire is written in. Would a student know what it is, let along what to do with it?"

"Interesting point. Yes, almost my entire grimoire is written in Latin. I inherited it from my paternal grandmother, who was Italian, and there are some Italian and Catalan spells from the eighteenth and nineteenth centuries as well."

CHAPTER 18

On Tuesday, Kelly gave me a ride to the college, and we walked by my apartment on my way to my first lecture. The doorway was still a shambles. But when I rushed from my lecture course back to my lab to meet with my graduate students that afternoon, two men were clearing debris away from the doorway, and the yellow police tape was gone.

I was surprised to find Lieutenant Kagan at the lab, chatting with the grad students as well as the girls who worked in the greenhouse. He broke away from them when he saw me approach.

"I spoke with Mrs. Bosun," he said, "and the door should be repaired this afternoon."

"Yes, there were some men working on it already. Thank you."

I told the students to give me fifteen minutes, then led Kagan into my apartment through the back door. I placed my new briefcase on the desk, then headed to the kitchen.

"Lemonade, Lieutenant?"

"Sure. Thank you."

He stood in the doorway, leaning on the jamb, while I poured a glass for each of us.

"You didn't find any grimoires or computers in Corey Lindsay's room, did you?" I asked.

"No. I was hoping you might let me search your lab and the greenhouse. Maybe his girlfriend hid them."

"Not that I can find. I searched this weekend. But maybe you can find something I couldn't. You have my permission."

Kagan pursed his mouth, then said, "I should have figured."

"Have you tried any magical techniques?" I asked. "You know, like scrying to find Kavanaugh's killer?"

He shook his head. "Nothing like that would be admissible in court."

I wanted to roll my eyes, but resisted. "Not in a mundane court. But at least it might give you a direction."

"I'll run it by the chief. He's a witch, so maybe he'll go for it. Something like that is beyond my talents, though."

"Not my strong point either, but we offer divination courses here on campus, so I assume there are people who might be able to help."

Wicklow College had the deepest repository of arcane talents outside the Witches' Council, but the local cops wanted to play Poirot and not use us. And I had thought students were the densest material in the universe.

After Kagan left, I quickly changed clothes and went back to the lab. The girls who worked in the greenhouse were waiting for me in the herb garden.

"What happened to your door?" Ava Martinez asked.

"There was an accident. A student experiment gone wrong, I think."

"Aren't you afraid?" Barbara asked.

"Why should I be afraid?"

The girl stared down at her feet. "Well, Dr. Kavanaugh and Ms. Bishop were murdered, and someone tried to blow you up."

I tried to chuckle, but my mouth was too dry. "I don't think any of those things are connected. I didn't know Dr. Kavanaugh or Ms. Bishop, and I've been here only a couple of weeks. No one has seen any of my exams yet, so I don't think anyone has a reason to harm me. I think that was a prank gone wrong."

"No exams, but your reading lists are pretty hefty," one of the graduate students said from the lab doorway.

I forced a smile and a laugh. "I'm devoted to my students. I don't want anyone thinking they aren't getting their money's worth. Besides, if anyone told you that graduate students have a social life, they lied."

A different voice from inside said, "Great, we'll all die old maids."

I urged the undergrads to get back to work and led the graduate students into the lab.

"There are worse fates than dying as old maids, as long as you don't die as sacrificed virgins. Let's explore socially acceptable ways of dealing with headaches. As you can see by my presence here today, blowing up your professors doesn't always work. Miss Simmons, tell us everything you know about willow bark."

⁂

Steven was sprawled on my back steps when the tutorial finished, providing a visual dessert for the students as they left.

"Hey, what's up?" I unlocked the back door to my apartment and grinned at the gawking young women streaming past as I ushered him inside.

"Flying back to San Francisco tonight. Talked to Carver today, and he understands that I have to deal with my apartment there and bring my car out here. So, I have an extra week."

"Tonight?"

"Yeah. Taxi is supposed to pick me up in about half an hour. I stashed my suitcase in my new apartment. I didn't see any reason to haul it there just to haul it back. Do you think you can manage to survive until I get back?"

Steven's on-campus studio apartment was free but even smaller than his place in San Francisco. Basically, it was a one-third size version of mine, without the garden view. When I saw it, I once again marveled at my luck.

"I'll try. You're probably smart not to be seen with me too often. You could end up a target, too."

"Savanna, what in the hell is going on here?"

"I truly wish I knew. I think it has something to do with a book called the Gambler Grimoire. If you can sniff out anything about it on the West Coast, I'd appreciate it." I proceeded to tell him what little I knew about the book.

Steven looked thoughtful. "An old buddy of mine lives in Vegas. I'll give him a call."

A car horn beeped from outside.

"Probably my taxi. See you in a couple of weeks."

I saw him to the door and watched as he trotted to the taxi waiting out front.

The door. Two shiny new keys sat on the table in the entrance hall, and I tried both on the new door. When I finished the experiment, I locked up, and used the lipstick in my purse to sketch runes on both sides of the door so I could cast a warding spell. Then I set off for the Faculty Club dining room.

On my way there, I reflected that perhaps I should call a few of my own contacts as well.

"Savanna, the Gambler Grimoire is just one of a group of fabled spell books that people are mad to find. Surely, you've come across tales of spells that will actually turn lead to gold," my father said when I called him.

"Yes, and with a nuclear reactor, I might be able to pull it off. Those ancient alchemists didn't understand atomic theory. Or how absolutely inert lead is."

"And I would guess that probability is as easily altered."

"But, Dad, it doesn't have to actually work for someone to believe enough—or hope—it does to kill for it."

"True. I've seen people do some pretty stupid things. I'll ask around, but you be careful. This fictitious book might have started the mess you're dealing with, but it sounds as though things have progressed. Whether the book is real or not may not be as important as a killer trying to cover up his tracks."

I stared at the phone after hanging up. Four deaths, assuming Merriweather was connected to the Wicklow murders. Even though Kagan thought Joshua Tupper's murder was unrelated to Brett Kavanaugh's, I didn't buy it. Coincidence was the one kind of magic I had trouble believing in.

And where would someone stash a bunch of computers?

Picking up the phone again, I called Kelly.

"Do students all provide their own computers?" I asked when she answered.

"Mostly, although we have a set of specifications they have to meet. Otherwise, they can buy them through the bookstore at a discount, compared to online or the store in town."

"And if something goes wrong, who fixes them?"

"Oh, I have a couple of techs working for me. If your computer glitches, bring it to the library. The workshop is in the back of the bookstore."

The following morning, I stopped by the computer repair shop on my way to my office. A young man with shoulder-length hair and a beard, wearing a t-shirt and jeans, came to the counter.

"Hi, what can I do for you?"

I looked around. Shelves holding laptop computers covered every wall. It appeared that each one had a tag attached to it. More equipment was stacked under the workbenches. An open doorway led to another room, and from what I could see, it was a duplicate of the front room.

"Are all these here for repair?" she asked.

"Yeah, most of them. Some are beyond hope, and I just haven't bundled them up for disposal yet. Some are loaners."

"And who has access back there?"

He cocked his head. "Me, a couple of students who work for me, and Ms. Grace, my boss. Who are you?"

"Oh, I'm sorry. Dr. Robinson, Alchemy and Apothecary Arts. I'm Dr. Kavanaugh's replacement. I was just wondering about his computer—wondering what might have become of it."

He shook his head. "No idea. As far as I know, it was never here, except once last winter. When he first bought it, he brought it in to get some software installed."

With a last look around, I thanked him and left. Considering the jumble of equipment—dozens of computers, printers, cords, and boxes I didn't know the purpose of—I had my doubts that anyone knew exactly what was in the shop, or where any specific thing was. But if the library was a good place to hide a book, the computer repair shop would be a good place to hide a computer.

On my way out, I stopped by Kelly's office and found her in.

"Hi. Is this the only library on campus? I mean, are there other places books are kept?"

"Good morning. I think you'll find books in most of the labs and work spaces. You have some in your lab, don't you?"

"Dr. Kavanaugh had some books there, yes. Standard

alchemical manuals and basic spell books. A few chemistry books."

Kelly nodded. "That's the sort of thing I mean. There's a reading room in graduate student housing. I have no idea what's there. The books should be under my control, but I don't have the manpower to staff the room twenty-four hours a day."

"Who has access to it?"

"Everyone. There isn't even a door on the room. Are you still thinking about those grimoires?"

"And the computers."

"Good luck. It's on the third floor of the north wing."

On my way back to my apartment that afternoon, I ventured into the building Kelly had mentioned and took the stairs to the third floor. I wandered down the hall until I came to a room without a door.

Sticking my head in, I saw it was a bare room with three tables, eight chairs, and shelves, made from lumber and cinder blocks, lining the walls. The tables had several stacks of books on them, and the shelves held lots of books—stacked or shelved. Some of the shelved books were backwards, with their pages rather than the spines pointed outward. The trash can had a couple of pizza boxes in it.

I wandered around the room, looking at the books and titles. They ranged from textbooks to academic treatises to fiction and pornography. I found an ancient copy of the Kama Sutra on one shelf. There wasn't any order that I could discern. Peeking into the bathroom, I found a short stack of books on top of the toilet tank.

A large number of the books radiated magic, so it would have taken me hours to go through them to determine whether any grimoires were present. Perhaps Kelly could search the room quicker.

CHAPTER 19

A knock on my door at seven in the morning revealed Kelly Grace, looking about half awake.

"Do you have coffee? I forgot to go to the store yesterday."

I smiled. "I can make some, or give you a strong cup of Assam tea."

"I'll take anything. I'm dragging this morning. My mum called at an ungodly hour, and I wasn't able to go back to sleep."

I led her back to the kitchen and poured a cup of tea to set in front of her. "Banana bread?"

Kelly sniffed once, then said, "Please. Mum said they had a visit at the shop. Two men she described as thugs, accompanied by a," she dropped into a very strong British accent, "very proper upper-class English gentleman—a witch. He wanted to know about the Gambler Grimoire. Told Mum and Aunt Celia that Uncle Harold had held an auction for the book, and he paid thirty thousand pounds for it. Then Harold died, but this guy still wants his book."

"And it took him six months to get around to asking for it?"

"Mmm-hmmm. Anyway, the shop was broken into later that

night, and among the things missing was the folder with Harold's and Brett's correspondence."

"Lovely."

"Worse. The shop was warded, and whoever broke in bypassed the wards. Savanna, my mum and her sister are getting up in years, but they aren't slouches. If they warded something, they have decades of practice keeping their kids out of things."

I laughed. I was as close to her mother's age as I was to hers. "Yeah, us old girls can still cast a spell or two."

"You're not old."

"Assuming your mom's online biography is correct, she's twelve years older than me, and I'm eleven years older than you."

Kelly took a sip of her tea. "You don't look it."

"I feel it, especially in the mornings and when I stand in front of a class. I'm old enough to be the mother of most of those kids."

Kelly chuckled. "They do look younger—and dumber—every year. But, do you think those guys in London will come here?"

I sat, took a bite of the warm bread, and sipped my tea. "No idea, but if he thinks thirty grand—that's what? About forty-five thousand dollars?—is worth breaking into the shop, then it's probably worth a trip to the middle of nowhere. I don't suppose your mom and aunt have a picture of these guys."

"Actually, they do. Uncle Harold didn't own a computer, but CCTV is ubiquitous in London. I'll have Mum send me a pic. You got up and baked this this morning?"

"Your mother wouldn't approve. It's from a mix."

"She would if the mix had her name on it. Oh, that reminds me. Mum said that you had some items on consignment with Uncle Harold?"

"Yes, I did. He occasionally sold a few things for me. I had forgotten. I sent them to him almost a year ago."

"Well, she said he sold them, but she can't find any record of him sending you any money."

"He was always slow about that."

"What kind of things did he sell for you? I assume something you made with your alchemy."

"Yes. I'm a wandsmith. I sent him five custom-made wands. You know something, I haven't heard a thing about Brett Kavanaugh's wand, either. Once he died, it could be re-bound to a new user."

Although I knew it would take someone at least two or three days to reach Wicklow, Pennsylvania, from London, I caught myself looking over my shoulder all day. The images in my mind from Kelly's tale involved hulking palookas with shaved heads and broken noses, and I was well aware of my physical limitations. Fear of muggers in San Francisco was the reason I developed the habit of carrying my wand everywhere I went.

There wasn't any reason for the book buyer in London to associate me with Brett Kavanaugh, or with the grimoire. If he and his minions did come to Wicklow, who would he target? With Kavanaugh dead, the mysterious witch in London would be in the same boat as Kagan, me, or anyone else curious about the book.

A week after my conversation with Kelly, I was walking from my office to my apartment when I noticed a man leaning against the wall, directly under Brett Kavanaugh's window. He was obviously trying to be discreet, but he stood out due to his age, his dress, and the fact that no one ever hung around outside the faculty apartments. Due to the college's wards, strangers were a rarity.

"May I help you?" I called when I got within about ten feet

of him. He appeared to be in his forties, slender, wearing khaki trousers, a V-neck sweater, rough heavy shoes, and a flat cap. He hadn't picked up a razor that morning, or had a recent haircut. In general, he appeared rumpled.

"Uh, no. Just waitin' for a friend," he said in a thick, lower-class British accent.

I shifted my briefcase to my left hand and reached inside my sleeve, taking my wand in hand.

"Who? Perhaps I can give you directions."

"He said to wait here. He should be along any time now."

"I see." I walked past him, keeping track of him from the corner of my eye, and pulled out my phone. I had the campus police on speed-dial, so I punched that button.

When someone answered, I said, "Hi, this is Professor Robinson. There's a strange man hanging around the faculty apartments, right under Professor Kavanaugh's apartment. He doesn't look like he belongs here."

"I'll send someone right away."

By the time I reached the end of the breezeway where my apartment was, two uniformed campus cops trotted up the stairs toward me. Turning and looking back the way I'd come, I saw two more policemen approaching the stranger.

I paused, watching, then opened my door and went inside. I closed the door, then watched through the scrying glass I had set up to watch the breezeway as the officers escorted the man off campus. I noticed that as they walked by, the man shot a glance at my door, and I wondered if I'd made a mistake.

I hadn't been close enough to him to feel any magic, but a stranger shouldn't have been on campus alone. The wards hadn't stopped him, however. I debated calling Chief Crumley, but what would I tell him? *Oh, by the way, I've been investigating Kavanaugh's murder behind your back, but now it looks as though I might have bitten off too much.* The opinions of Crumley and

Kagan didn't worry me overmuch, but I didn't want Carver and Phillips to decide I was a problem child.

It turned out I didn't have to worry about contacting the chief of campus police. About an hour later, Crumley knocked on my door.

"Hi, come on in. Can I offer you something to drink? Some tea, perhaps?"

"Uh, no, thank you. I just wanted to touch base about that prowler you reported," the chief said.

"He told me he was waiting for someone."

Crumley snorted. "Told my officers the same thing. Waiting for Brett Kavanaugh. Also mentioned Kelly Grace's name."

"Who was he?"

"An Englishman named Rupert Higgs. We didn't really have anything on him, so we let him go, but warned him he could be arrested for trespassing."

I took a deep breath. "How did he get on campus? I was told everything inside the wall was warded."

With a rueful grin, Crumley said, "It is, but he's a witch. We have to create wards that keep the wrong people out, but let the right people in. Your keys and faculty ID card are amulets that let you pass most places. But admission to the grounds themselves is open to witches. Parents pay the bills, you know."

"Well, thanks for telling me. I wonder what he's really here for. He didn't look like someone who belonged here."

Crumley shook his head. "I have no idea, ma'am. Maybe Dr. Kavanaugh owed him some money. According to his passport, though, he's been in the country only a couple of days. It would have to be a lot of money to fly all the way here from England to collect it."

CHAPTER 20

"It's no secret that Harold Merriweather was my uncle, or that I work at Wicklow," Kelly said. "Maybe they tied me to my mum when they stole that correspondence between Uncle Harold and Brett." She took a deep breath and another swallow of wine. "Just what I need."

She had brought the pictures from the CCTV her mother had emailed from London. One of the 'thugs' was the same man I had seen the day before.

"Or," I said, "you were the only name at Wicklow they recognized when they came looking for Kavanaugh."

"They can't have done much research, or they'd know Brett is dead."

I shrugged. "Most criminals aren't geniuses. That's why they get caught. It does bother me how quickly they showed up here. The grimoire went missing at Christmas, and now there's a sudden urgency."

"Maybe there's a buyer."

"Yeah. Maybe I should check on the Witches' Web."

"Good luck. Don't look for it under that name or you'll get deluged with results," Kelly said. "Look for probability spells."

"You've looked."

"Yup. There's an offer of a hundred thousand bucks for the genuine article from a known billionaire collector. It's a standing offer that's two years old. Uncle Harold knew him. Why would he take less than half that much on an auction?"

"That might explain why Kavanaugh killed him. That price would have been a bit steep."

"I'm in the wrong business," Kelly said. "Mum and Aunt Celia asked me if I wanted to take over the shop. My talents are the right fit, but I just don't think I know enough to do it."

"How old was Harold?"

"About eighty. He'd been working in a bookshop since he was a teenager. Everyone knew him, and he had connections all over the world. I worked for him a couple of summers, but that was barely a superficial apprenticeship."

"Do you have an acquisitions budget?" I asked.

"Of course, I do. But even if Edmund—Dr. Phillips—approved, I'm not going to have a chance bidding against Trent McCarthy. He spends a hundred grand on dinner. He could buy our whole collection with petty cash." Kelly shrugged. "Of course, for all we know, the book is sitting under our noses, but we can't find it. Or, it's a myth, like David said, and we're chasing a unicorn."

I stood, walked to the window, and looked out over the garden. "I always wanted a unicorn, but Dad wouldn't buy me one. You know, I really don't care about the book, even if it's real. The fact that so many people are dying, and the book is implicated, is the only thing that makes me care about the book at all."

I turned to face Kelly, who was sitting across the room.

"I'm still having difficulty envisioning Brett Kavanaugh," I said. "There must have been more to him than being a womanizing collector of very strange artifacts. And I find it difficult to understand that a person could be here more than twenty years and have only a couple of friends."

Kelly sighed. "Yes, I guess it's hard to describe a very complex person to a stranger. Brett was intelligent, witty, and smooth. An old-fashioned gentleman, with refined, old-fashioned tastes. Great sense of humor, very sociable when he wanted to be. He skied, kayaked, and he had a very expensive mountain bike that's chained to a rack near his apartment."

"So, you saw him socially?"

"We traveled in some of the same social circles. He also liked to hang out at a bar near the Wayfarer Inn sometimes, The Shillelagh. Good for some Irish music and a pint of stout. Brett liked to put on airs, but he came from a working-class family."

I frowned. "I was told his family had money."

"They did, but his father earned it all in the restaurant business."

The next time I saw Katy, I asked, "Do you know who Dr. Kavanaugh was seeing at the time he died?"

Katy shook her head. "No idea. He and Kelly Grace had an on-off relationship for years, and he introduced me to a woman around Christmas last year. We ran into them at a restaurant one night, but I can't remember her name. Slender, young, with dark hair. Very pretty. But that was his type. I wondered at the time if she might be a student, but I think she was a little older than that. He sometimes kept two or three women on a string at the same time."

"Kelly?"

Katy winked. "I think she likes older men. Brett, Dr. Phillips, Dr. Ricard, Dr. Aubert. Nothing wrong with that, of course. She's a very pretty woman, and she attracts men."

I had briefly met Louis Aubert, professor of Alchemy, whose office was next to Ricard's.

I grinned and raised an eyebrow. "Is there anyone she hasn't been linked with?"

With a shrug, Katy said, "I really shouldn't gossip. Oftentimes gossip doesn't have much of a basis in fact, just nasty people being mean."

Out of curiosity, I went back to my office and pulled up the faculty and staff rosters on my computer. Other than me, there were only seven other unmarried women on the faculty, and I was the youngest. On staff, a larger number of younger women were single, including Kelly. Most of them were in clerical or administrative support positions. One was the head of Human Resources, but since I was hired without ever meeting her, I realized what importance the college put on the position.

Of course, there weren't many single men on the faculty, either, and a number of them were almost ancient.

When I headed home that afternoon after my last class, I found myself walking with Ophelia.

"Hi," I said, "going home or to work?"

"Work," the young woman answered. "I can hide out in the greenhouse, then hit the dining hall just before it closes. Honestly, Dr. Robinson, I never understood how vicious the rumor mill can be. Even my friends seem anxious to jump on me."

"I'm so sorry to hear that. I know that Lieutenant Kagan thinks there's something suspicious about me reporting two murders. As though I had something to do with them, or somehow planned on being there at that time."

Ophelia nodded. "I don't know what to do. My lawyer says I could end up in prison, and I didn't do anything!"

"As an accomplice?"

The girl took a deep breath. "Yes. Because I didn't turn Corey in. I mean, I understand right and wrong, and why you're supposed to report a crime. But Kagan seems to think I should have called the police on my own boyfriend! It was Josh's fault, not Corey's."

"Are you saying that Corey's guilty of killing Josh?" I asked.

"It was self-defense, but I shouldn't say anymore." Ophelia walked faster, but since I was taller, I didn't have any trouble matching her pace.

"This may sound cold," I said as we reached the breezeway leading past her apartment, "but you really need to think about yourself. Take care of Lia, and then worry about Corey."

"You sound like my lawyer. And my father."

"What you're hearing is common sense. You can't help anyone unless you're free to talk."

I stopped when we reached my door, and Ophelia also stopped.

"Dr. Robinson, I get the feeling that Kagan thinks I'm guilty—of something—but he's treated me that way since the first time he talked to me, and that was before Josh died."

I considered what to say. "I think he believes Dr. Kavanaugh might have been dating a student."

Ophelia stared at me in disbelief, then burst out laughing. "Me? That is rich! Believe me, he barely ever looked at me. Try someone a lot prettier. More athletic. Someone like your friend Ms. Grace or Emma was more his type."

Her eyes shifted to something past my shoulder, and her laughter cut off. I glanced that direction and saw Emma walking toward us.

"Hey, Lia," Emma called. "How are you doing?"

When Emma reached us, Ophelia turned and fell in step with her. I watched them walk away, down the steps to the street, and turn left toward the greenhouse. They could have been sisters, one taller, more slender, prettier, and more athletic than the other.

On the other side of the wall surrounding the campus, past the street, the man from England leaned against a tree by the parking lot that bordered the river. I unlocked my door and went inside.

CHAPTER 21

"That's him!" Kelly said, nudging me with her elbow.

"The love of your life?" I asked, looking up from the menu I was perusing. "Or even better, the love of *my* life?"

The expression on Kelly's face wasn't one of amusement.

"The man from London. The one Mum described as a gentleman."

I followed the line of Kelly's gaze and saw the man sitting next to the window. The Shillelagh had little to distinguish itself from most English or Irish pubs in North America, which was a large part of its charm on a Saturday morning. The man Kelly was watching was deeply immersed in destroying a full-Irish breakfast.

"He does give the impression of class," I said, noting the quality and cut of his suit. I took a picture of the guy with my phone, thinking it wouldn't hurt to have one.

The waitress showed up about that time.

"I don't think I can do the whole thing," I said. "I'll take the half breakfast."

Kelly chuckled. "The full-Irish for me, with orange juice and more coffee."

The waitress picked up the menus and left.

"You may regret not topping up," Kelly said. She had talked me into another kayaking excursion that day.

"We'll see who floats better. So, he has to know that Kavanaugh's dead, and it's been a week since the police escorted his buddy off campus, but he's still hanging around. Maybe we should follow him and see if he finds the grimoire."

"Have fun," Kelly responded. "Personally, I don't care who has it, as long as things settle back to normal and I don't have to worry about people dying."

Since the man had arrived at the pub before Kelly and me, he obviously wasn't following either of us. But I was still curious.

"I wonder where he's staying."

Kelly gave an indifferent shrug. "The Wayfarer, or the Grand. Other than those two, chain motels are about the only choices. He doesn't look like the chain motel type."

I agreed. Most tourists in Wicklow were more of the outdoorsy types, not those who wore a three-piece suit to breakfast on Saturday morning.

"Are there any arcane bookstores in Wicklow?" It seemed strange that I hadn't thought to ask that before.

"Not really. Not like Merriweather's, but Carragher's carries some books on the arcane and the occult, and Agnes had a little room in the back with some books."

***

When we got back to town after the kayak trip, I had Kelly drop me off downtown.

"I'll walk home. I want to do a little browsing around," I told her.

Kelly laughed. "Carragher's is on Fourth Street, about a block off Main. They close at six."

I shook my head. Other than bars, restaurants, and gas stations, it seemed as though everything in Wicklow closed early. After living in San Francisco for so long, it took some getting used to, and Kelly was constantly having to remind me that Wicklow wasn't a twenty-four-hour town.

The first place I went to was Back to Basics to see Iris Bishop. A 'Grand Re-Opening' banner hung across the front of the shop, and a couple of small chalkboards on the sidewalk advertised specials. At mid-afternoon, there was a healthy crowd inside the shop.

Iris did have some help—a woman working the cash register. Based on descriptions I had heard, I wondered if the woman was Helen Donnelly.

I browsed through the shop, found the nook with books, and saw nothing of interest. I did pick up an oven glove, a couple of dish towels, an assortment of dried herbs in plastic bags, and a tea infuser. I waited until Iris and the other woman were alone at the register, then approached them.

"Your re-opening seems to be going fairly well," I said, putting my purchases on the counter.

"Hi!" Iris said. "Yes, business has been good. I don't plan to carry a lot of stuff Agnes had in her stock, so I put it all on sale. Do you know Helen?"

"I haven't had the pleasure," I said. "I'm Savanna Robinson. Helen Donnelly, I take it?"

The Donnelly woman smiled at first, but the smile left her face when I identified myself. I paid, and as Iris bagged my goods, pulled out my phone.

"You wouldn't happen to have run into this gentleman, would you?" I asked, turning the phone toward the two women.

They both peered at the picture. Iris smiled. "Oh, yes. He stopped by yesterday. Said that he knew Agnes from years ago. Very pleasant. Expressed his condolences and asked if I knew why she had been murdered. Wondered if it was a robbery or something. He asked about grimoires, but of course, Agnes carried only those gardening books back there and some silly books on pseudo witchcraft."

She looked up from the phone. "That reminds me. Lieutenant Kagan said that they didn't find Agnes's grimoire. I've looked all over for it. I don't suppose she might have left it in her office on campus?"

I shook my head. "No. The girls who work in the greenhouse say that she always took it with her. That's the odd thing. Two murders, and although I'm told that both Dr. Kavanaugh and Agnes had grimoires handed down through their families, both books are missing."

Helen's head jerked up. "Brett's spell book is missing?"

"So I'm told," I said, giving the woman a smile. "Of course, I came along after his death and never met the man, so I really don't know. I'm just curious about why so many people die around here." I raised an eyebrow at Iris. "It's like moving into a war zone, or a TV mystery show."

Iris nodded.

"It's just a weird coincidence that you moved here at the same time as a murder," Helen said.

"Or there's a homicidal maniac on the loose," I responded, then picked up my bags, and left the store.

It was a six-block walk to Fourth Street. I turned right when I got there and saw a sign 'Books' halfway down the block. I stopped, looked back the way I had come, and chuckled. The man the police had removed from campus was watching me from across Main Street. The man Kelly and I had seen at breakfast was half a block behind me. I didn't spot the third man Kelly's mum had sent a picture of.

Proceeding down the street, I looked in the windows of the bookstore—across the top of the window was painted, 'Carragher's New and Used Books'—then went inside. The man behind the counter was reading a book and glanced over the top of his glasses at me. A gray fringe encircled his bald head, his long hair pulled back in a short ponytail. His beard was neatly trimmed, and he wore a bright blue Hawaiian shirt. The book he was reading was David Hume's *Moral Philosophy*.

I glanced around the shop, taking in the way it was laid out, and how the books and book categories were presented. Best sellers at the front, of course, but the shelves on the walls near the front had a healthy serving of fiction—romance, science fiction, and fantasy. Books on Pennsylvania—geography, history, and tourist attractions—were a little farther back.

"Excuse me," I said, approaching the counter. "I'm Dr. Savanna Robinson. I just started teaching at the college, and I hoped you might carry some books I would be interested in."

The man slowly lowered his book, raised his eyes, and gave me a thorough inspection.

"Lowell Carragher. I guess that would depend on whether you were looking for books in your academic field, or a romance to fill your evening."

"I'm more of a sword-and-sorcery kind of girl."

His mouth twisted into a grin. "Heavy on the sorcery? Around the corner, or over there." He motioned to what appeared to be a hallway with a 'Restrooms' sign hanging above it, then to the science fiction section. "Take a right, and then another one."

"Thank you."

The books in the small room he directed me to included some I might consider for a serious academic reading list. I picked up a basic apothecary book that I already owned, thinking to put it in the lab rather than my own copy, which had scribblings in the margins. After another half an hour looking around the store, I took the book to the counter.

"You wouldn't happen to be interested in grimoires, would you?" Carragher asked.

"What makes you ask that?"

"The company you keep," he said, his eyes flashing briefly toward the front of the store. Outside, one of the men following me watched the store from across the street, the other was pretending to look at the books in the window.

"Oh, of course. Do you have any spell books that require an exotic accent? I've been hunting forever for one written in either Cockney or Glaswegian."

He snorted a laugh.

"We told them at the college that Brett Kavanaugh doesn't live here anymore, but they're still hanging around. Unfortunately, they seem to have attached themselves to me this afternoon."

"I'm getting ready to close up for the day. If you like, I'd be glad to escort you to your car."

I smiled at him. "That's awfully sweet of you, but since I don't have a car, it would be a rather long walk."

"I could offer you a ride, but it might be quicker to walk to your place. I live about five blocks from here and didn't bring my car today."

"My apartment is on campus. But I don't think I have anything to fear from them."

"They just strike me as a rough crowd."

I turned and studied the men outside. "Well, thank you. I do appreciate it, but I have a bit of shopping to do, then I'll take the bus."

I paid for the book, tucked it into one of the bags from the other store, and walked to the grocery store. The men from England were nowhere in sight. Iris's shop was still open, and she still had customers. I hoped people were drawn to the sale, rather than by macabre curiosity, but didn't delude myself.

Later, standing at the bus stop with my bag of groceries and watching the sunset, I was startled by a voice, speaking in a cultured British accent.

"You could earn a very handsome finder's fee for a certain grimoire."

I turned, smiled, and batted my eyes. "I'm sure the same could be said if I discovered a cure for cancer. Tell me why I would give either one to you instead of selling them directly."

The crunch of a footstep on gravel alerted me that the nicely dressed Englishman and I weren't alone.

"It would be far safer to let someone more experienced handle the book."

"How kind of you. You're probably right. A woman shouldn't worry herself about such weighty matters."

"Quite right."

There was a faint stirring of the air behind me, the scuff of a shoe on the sidewalk, an indeterminate feeling that someone had entered my personal space. I bent over and set my bags on the ground. When I straightened, I stepped away from both men while pulling my wand from my sleeve.

The man behind and to my left stepped toward me. I took another step back while whipping my wand out into the space between us. He was a little too slow, and the wand slashed across his chest in a burst of tiny stars.

"*Glacio!*" I cried. Both men froze where they stood.

"Quite impressive."

I whirled about to find Lowell Carragher standing fifteen feet away. He was taller than I had thought he would be.

"Perhaps, but I have no idea what to do with them now. The bus will be here any minute."

"Is that spell figurative or literal?" Carragher asked.

"Literal, I'm afraid. I didn't plan ahead. They won't survive very long once their blood finishes freezing."

Carragher walked over and touched one man's cheek with his fingertips. "Ah, yes, quite frosty. You do know what they seek, don't you?"

I nodded. "They tried to intimidate people in London for information a week or so ago, then broke into Merriweather's."

"And obviously didn't find what they were looking for."

"They stole some correspondence between Harold Merriweather and Brett Kavanaugh. I assume that's why they're in Wicklow."

"That makes some sense. You're friends with Kelly, I presume. There's your bus. I would be fascinated to continue this conversation. Dinner some evening, perhaps?"

"What do I do about these idiots?"

"Just leave them here. Release the spell when you get on the bus."

"What about you?"

Carragher smiled. "I don't think I'll have any more trouble with them than you did. Call me at the store."

The bus pulled up, I hastily snatched up my bags, showed the driver my bus pass, and muttered, "*Inrita.*" As the bus drove away, I saw Carragher and the man in the suit standing and talking to each other.

CHAPTER 22

David Hamilton met me at the bottom of the steps leading from the street to our apartments. He reached for one of the bags of groceries.

"I'm really not as helpless as you seem to think," I said, surrendering the bag.

"Looks like you have your hands full."

I opened my door, then snatched my groceries away from him.

"Do you know Lowell Carragher? Well, I assume you know him, the size of this town and all. I mean do you know him very well?"

"Yes, we go fishing quite often. Why?"

"Was he friends with Brett Kavanaugh?"

"He was. He's also good friends with Kelly Grace and Anton Ricard. And probably most of the faculty here. He teaches an occasional course, and works with the bookstore to help us order books. Why?"

I took a deep breath, glanced down at the bags in my arms, and said, "Do you have a little time? Would you like to come in and have a drink?"

David followed me into my apartment and took a seat in the living room while I put my groceries away and came back with two glasses of wine.

It took me about half an hour to tell him about the men confronting Loretta Grace and her sister in London, and the men's appearance in Wicklow.

When I finished, I said, "That's why I was asking about Lowell Carragher."

Hamilton was quiet for a few minutes, shifting his gaze from his wine glass to me, then to the view out my window.

"Lowell is all right," he finally said. "I would trust him with my life, if that were necessary. A very strong witch, especially adept at manipulating nature. And if Brett did have the Gambler Grimoire, and had questions about it, then Lowell is who he probably would have spoken to. But as far as money is concerned, Lowell has no need for money, at least in the amounts you've mentioned. If he was interested in the book, it would be for the content, not as a business product."

"I've always found that people say they aren't interested in money until they have a chance to get some."

He shrugged. "Since he owns that entire block where his store is located downtown, as well as the shopping center on the west bank of the river, and a resort north of the city—with no debt on any of it—I feel fairly confident that a hundred grand isn't going to entice him too much. He and Harold Merriweather were friends, so he might know about the book."

Swallowing the last of his wine, he added, "I'm concerned about these guys from England. Did they physically accost you?"

"Not really. I never let either of them get close enough to actually touch me, but I did feel threatened. I prefer not to engage in mage battles in the middle of downtown. I mean, there were people around, families and kids."

"You froze them? I mean, actually froze them with cold?

You blinded me, froze them, what other kind of goodies do you have up your sleeve?"

I sighed. "I'm not a very subtle sort of girl. Oh, I could fight fire with fire, ice with ice, and some of my students think my sarcasm should be classified as a deadly weapon. I'm not going to start any earthquakes or call any tornadoes. I should have used the spell that Kelly used on you. The one I used was probably a bit too dangerous, but them following me around all day just put my teeth on edge, and maybe I wanted to frighten them a little."

After David left, I took a shower, fixed dinner, then called the number listed on the internet for Carragher's bookstore. Since it was after dark, I didn't expect anyone to answer, but Lowell surprised me.

"This is Savanna Robinson."

"Good evening, pretty lady. Are you doing okay?"

"I'm fine, flatterer. My next-door neighbor tells me that you might know more about that grimoire than you let on today."

"And who's your neighbor?"

"David Hamilton."

"Can't believe anything he says about me. He's jealous because I catch more fish than he does."

I laughed. "I'll remember that. He said you were honest. What's the difference between the truth and a fisherman's tale?"

"Usually about sixteen inches for the fish around here. Are you free for dinner tomorrow evening?"

"What did you discuss with those men after I left?"

"I was just trying to get an idea of how much they were willing to pay for you. We don't get many human traffickers in Wicklow, so I'm not familiar with current prices. Turns out they're cheapskates. For that kind of money, I'd rather keep you for myself. My time is better spent sweet-talking you into going to dinner with me and solving the riddle."

"And what riddle is that?"

"Who killed Brett Kavanaugh, and is there really a book that can make us all rich before we're the next ones killed."

I thought about that answer. "Do you really think the book is the reason he was murdered?"

"Makes as much sense as trying to figure out which jealous husband did it. To be honest, Dr. Robinson, I'd be ashamed if I couldn't be more creative than Sam Kagan in looking for a motive."

"Call me Savanna. And you think the two of us can figure it all out?"

I heard him snort a laugh. "Oh, hell no. But you're the prettiest girl to move into town since Kelly Grace, and you're a lot closer to my age than she is."

"I'm not sure if that's a compliment."

"It is."

"Do you know where David lives?"

"Yes, I do."

"I'm directly across the breezeway, first floor. What time?"

"Six o'clock."

"How should I dress?"

"Like the queen of San Francisco when she ventures out among the Pennsylvania peasants. I shall see you then." He hung up, leaving me staring at the phone and wondering what I had agreed to.

I immediately placed a call to Kelly. "Tell me about Lowell Carragher."

Kelly's laughter sounded joyful. "Did he ask you out?"

"Why do you ask that?"

"He's an incurable flirt. He's asked me to marry him about fifty times."

"He's old enough to be your father."

"So I've told him, but he just leers, winks, and says he doesn't consider that a problem, then makes some tired joke about aging producing the finest wine."

"And vinegar. Another player," I said with a sigh.

"Not really. At least with me, I know he's not serious, but he's one of those men who flirts with every woman—old, young, pretty or not, married or single—but no one takes him seriously. Or almost no one. I understand that he and Katy Bosun were high school sweethearts, but then she met her husband. It's part of his charm, and everyone shops at his place instead of the big chain stores in Youngstown or Pittsburgh. Kids love him, and he does a reading circle for them on Wednesday evenings."

I recounted my afternoon and Lowell's intervention at the bus stop.

"Oh, I definitely trust him," Kelly said after I finished. "At least as far as telling me the truth. If I were you, though, I'm not sure I'd trust an invitation to see his etchings, and I'm not as sanguine as David is about whether Lowell would be interested in the book."

"He's probably not hitting on David," I said, "and I'm not entirely sure what David is interested in besides fish."

"And you."

That comment left me staring at the phone with my mouth open. "What would make you say that? I haven't picked up a single indication that he thinks about me at all."

"You don't know him very well. Just the fact that he pays any attention to you at all is unusual."

"We live next door to each other. He'd have to ignore me to the point of rudeness to acknowledge me any less."

"Whatever. The rumor is that he dated a woman years ago, but she had to make the first move. He's incredibly shy, and he hides it with brusqueness. The complete opposite of Brett or Lowell."

CHAPTER 23

I stood in front of my closet, pondering what the queen of San Francisco would wear to dinner with a strange man in Wicklow. I finally settled on a black dress—lace over satin with an irregular hemline, bloused sleeves, and a built-in corset—and knee-high boots. Very witchy. A silver brooch set with a large amethyst was my only jewelry, other than my wand, which I disguised as a belt.

Lowell was punctual, knocking on the door at exactly six o'clock. When I answered it, I found he was dressed much like my colleagues at the college—tweed jacket, khaki pants, and white open-collared shirt.

"Oh, my," he said. "My dear, you're stunning."

I felt my face burn. "Thank you. When we met, I had just returned from kayaking all day. Not my best look."

He escorted me to a battered Range Rover, and we drove back to town, through town, and out of town on the old river road going north.

"So, to where am I being kidnapped?" I asked.

"A better restaurant than any in Wicklow," he replied. "Special of the day is always fresh-caught Allegheny River fish."

"David said you owned a resort."

He grinned. "That I do, with my sister. Inherited from our parents. In warm weather, we cater to fishermen, hikers, and kayakers. We also have a stable. In winter, it's mainly cross-country skiers. It's not very fancy, and I don't make any money from it, but it pays the salary of a chef I couldn't afford otherwise, supports my sister, and puts my nieces and nephews through college. Best restaurant between Pittsburgh and Buffalo. Of course, the competition isn't littered with Michelin stars."

The river twisted and turned through the forest, and we passed through a small town.

"Are the other small towns around here witch-friendly?" I asked.

"Not really. Outside of Wicklow, it's best to keep a low profile. For the most part, people tend to ignore the college. And although we have a couple of big-box stores in West Wicklow, a lot of people in outlying areas go to Youngstown if they're going to travel to shop."

The road crossed a bridge across the river, and then another bridge over a smaller tributary, and Lowell steered the four-wheel-drive onto a paved driveway. The sign said, 'Carragher's Retreat.' I noted that it was close enough to the college that I could ride a bike out there on a weekend day. Assuming my new bicycle ever arrived.

A couple of hundred yards along a path with lights on both sides brought us to a well-lit building that was a cross between a nineteenth-century mansion and a timber-built lodge. There were thirty or forty cars in the parking lot.

"Looks like business is good," I said. Lowell's remark that the place wasn't 'very fancy' said a lot more about him than the resort.

"Most of these cars are either staff or dinner guests," Lowell said. "The real money comes from the resort guests. But if you're not able to dine at the Faculty Club, this is the place in Wicklow for special occasions. Birthdays, anniversaries, and we do a lot of weddings."

The maître 'd escorted us to a table by a window. The view of the sunset over the river was breathtaking.

"Was this the family homestead back in the good old days?" I asked.

"You are a very perceptive young lady. The barns and pastures are out back, but other than a couple of fields of alfalfa for the horses, we don't farm here anymore."

"We?"

"My sister and her family live here. She owns half the place and runs it. I get free meals as long as I don't try and tell anyone what to do. Her oldest boy is a student at Wicklow College, and her oldest girl is a student at Penn State."

"Did you go to Wicklow?"

"Yes, although I think my time at the University of Pittsburgh was better spent."

"Never married?"

"Nope. You?"

I grinned. "No one would have me."

Lowell nodded. "Far too intimidating, I imagine. You remind me of a woman who taught at the college ten, maybe twelve, years ago. All the men chased her, but I got the impression they weren't really as interested in catching her as they pretended to be. After a year, she left and never came back."

"You wouldn't happen to remember her name?"

"Sure. Catherine Walker. Dr. Catherine Walker. Freshly minted PhD. Oh, she was a pretty one. Like Kelly, and about that age when she was here."

"And you fell in love."

He chuckled. "Oh, not me. All the others—David and Brett and Anton and who knows how many of them. I got the impression they scared her off. She wasn't looking to get married and settle down, in my opinion." He leaned over the table and pointed to my menu. "If you like fish, order the walleye special. You won't regret it."

After the waiter took our orders, I asked, "So, you never fell in love?"

Lowell clasped his chest and gave me an affronted look. "Of course I did, but sweet Katy Malone stole my heart, and until I met you, I never found anyone to lessen the pain."

"You are too much," I said, laughing so hard I started coughing. After taking a sip of water, I asked, "Is that Katy Bosun?"

"The same. She's a few years younger than I am, and after I pined away for years waiting for her to grow up, she fell in love with another man."

"Tell me about Brett Kavanaugh and the Gambler Grimoire."

"Did you ever hear about the law of unintended consequences?"

"Once or twice."

"An old friend of my father used to tell a tale about a spell that would make all your problems go away. As soon as a witch cast it, they never had another problem, obstacle, or unhappy moment."

"Uh-huh. And?"

"It was a death spell. A suicide spell. The idea that magic can bend the laws of probability strikes me the same way. Be careful what you ask for."

I nodded. "I agree with you. I also have reservations about magic that attempts to change something abstract. What if my concept of something is different than the universe's concept, and I try to change it. The spell works, but the result is completely different than what I expect."

"That's almost a political or theological concept," Lowell said.

"Okay. Which theology is correct? Unless you're absolutely

sure that your world view is exactly how the world works, it's a little bit like walking on eggshells, isn't it? We have Christian witches, pagan witches, Hindu witches. Who's right?"

He leaned back in his chair and studied me. "I'll bet you're a demon in the classroom."

I winked at him. "Students are endlessly curious, and endlessly creative. If you're going to encourage critical thinking, you'd better be prepared before you let the genii out of the bottle. 'Because I said so,' or 'it's against the rules,' ain't gonna cut it. University students and three-year-olds have that 'why?' question down pat."

Lowell laughed. "Wine?"

"Who's driving us home?"

"I have a cabin here."

"That's nice for you. Do I need to register to get my own room? I hope there's a vacancy." I leaned forward. "You know, it's common courtesy to let a woman know when she's expected to bring her toothbrush."

"We have a shuttle that takes people back to town."

"Ah. So, I can get home without perusing your etchings? Will it still take me home after I murder you?"

His laughter was loud enough that everyone in the dining room turned to look at us. My face felt ready to ignite.

"My sister would probably consider your actions justified."

"Sauvignon blanc. Does that mean I could catch the shuttle to bring me out here for dinner?"

"It does. It runs through town from the Wayfarer three times each evening. The last run back into town leaves here at ten-thirty. But if you ask about it when you make reservations, it will pick you up at the college."

"You never did give me an honest answer as to what you discussed with those English thugs."

"No, I didn't. George Peterson is the man in charge of that lovely group. I've known him for some years. He brokers artifacts, and I know of at least one amulet that he sold to Brett. He tends to be unconcerned with the provenance of the items he deals with."

"And?"

"I told him that I might not be around to bail him out the next time you get angry."

"Not angry so much as frightened."

"That is a rather unusual wand you carry."

"Why is he so interested in that book?"

"He seems convinced it's the real deal—The Gambler Grimoire, as it's commonly known. He says it codifies the noetic sciences."

"Bah! Noetics is just another word for magic, and we've been codifying it for centuries. Only those who think the scientific study of magic is new spout that claptrap. Newton and da Vinci put paid to magic not having anything to do with science."

"That's a rather strong statement."

"Yes, it is, isn't it? But I just went down that rabbit hole with a couple of students in one of my tutorials. We bend the laws of physics; we don't rewrite them. And the concept of controlling the future, when we don't know what that future is, or the ramifications of changing it, strikes me as a little arrogant."

"Well, Brett Kavanaugh had that kind of arrogance. And so does Trent McCarthy, the man Peterson is working for."

"You know that Kavanaugh had the book?"

He shook his head. "I know he was interested in it. Harold Merriweather contacted me and told me he had it. I told Brett."

"And Brett cut out the middleman and went straight to Merriweather."

Lowell picked up the wine bottle and leaned forward to refill my glass. "It wasn't really like that. I didn't want anything to do with it, and the commission would have been so small as not to be worth it."

"We think Kavanaugh might have killed Merriweather for the book."

The look of surprise on Carragher's face didn't strike me as feigned.

"Do you know if he ever had it?" I asked.

Lowell shook his head, took a deep breath, and then a swallow of his wine. "No, not that he told me. I knew Harold died, but I thought it was from natural causes." He played with his glass a bit, staring at the liquid. "Of course, Brett was an apothecary, so that wouldn't have been difficult for him to fake."

"Whoever killed Harold Merriweather didn't use a very subtle poison. I think that's what surprises me most about this whole affair—the lack of subtlety. Aconite, fireplace pokers, athames, nitroglycerine, accosting women in the street. No one seems to have any appreciation for finesse."

The waiter appeared with our dinners, set them on the table, poured more wine, and went away.

"That may be true," Lowell said, "but so far no one has been caught for any of the crimes."

"Unless you consider the possibility that we have a daisy-chain of murders. Everyone who's been caught is dead. Who's next?"

CHAPTER 24

It still bothered me that neither Kagan, Chief Crumley, or anyone else had considered scrying Kavanaugh's murder, not to mention Agnes Bishop's or Joshua Tupper's. Postcognition spells were difficult but not impossible. Considering the number of witches in the area, and the skills represented at the college, I couldn't understand why no one had made the attempt.

Tupper's killing was supposedly solved, although the reason for it was still shrouded. The sheer number of people who had been in Agnes's shop since her death probably precluded any chance of picking up the psychic residuals of her murder. But although Kavanaugh's apartment had finally been cleaned, no one had moved in, and very few people had been in the place.

That type of scrying wasn't one of my strong talents, so I knew I would need help in casting such a spell. Considering the mixed messages and interpretations I was getting from people in Wicklow, I decided to wait until Steve returned from the West Coast. He was the one person I felt completely confident couldn't have killed Brett Kavanaugh.

But there was one area of curiosity I could pursue in the

meantime. Katy Bosun mentioning the love quadrangle had triggered a question in the back of my mind, and Lowell had answered the question for me.

It had been ten years since Catherine Walker and I were roommates in Santa Cruz, but we had run into each other occasionally at conferences or other events. After I got home from dinner with Lowell, I dialed the number I had for her and sat back while it rang. If Catherine was still on the West Coast, it would be early evening there.

"Hello?"

"Cat? Savanna Robinson."

"Well, long time. What are you up to?"

"Ever heard of a place called Wicklow College?"

"You're kidding, right? One of the worst years of my life was spent teaching there."

"It does have its charms. You're a legend here, you know? Are you still in Santa Cruz?"

A dry, humorless laugh. "I'll bet. Seriously? You should have called before you took the job, but it's been a long time. The people I had trouble with are probably all gone. Yeah, I'm a tenured full professor and department head." The Institute of Witchcraft at Santa Cruz was a smaller college, situated in the redwoods, and very laid back.

"Remember a Brett Kavanaugh?"

"God's gift to women? Royal pain in the ass? Yeah, I remember him. He giving you trouble?"

"In an abstract way. He was murdered, and I got his job."

"That's a little extreme, Savanna. Academia is supposed to be cut-throat only in a metaphorical sense."

"That's what I thought. Who else gave you problems?"

"A guy named Jerome Carver. Married, but the absolute octopus king of sexual harassment. The only man I ever wanted to turn into a toad. Louis Aubert. Backstabbing son of a bitch. Stole a paper I wrote and submitted it to a journal as his own work. Anton Ricard. His problem was persistence, and the fact he took Aubert's side in our dispute. I haven't trusted a French-Canadian since. Anton and Brett couldn't get it through their heads that I wasn't interested."

"Anyone you were interested in?"

A sigh. "Yeah. David Hamilton. Is he still there? I don't think I ever chased a man that hard. I practically had to hit him over the head and drag him home. You know, he's the only person from that time I ever think about. And my apartment. I had a lovely old place with a private entrance to the college's herb garden."

"He's still here. Still single, and still sexy."

Another sigh. "I'm not. Single, I mean. Probably not sexy, either. I've been living with a guy for almost five years now. We're talking about spawning."

"The spawn of Catharine. It could be a movie."

"A very boring one, nowadays. My older sister, Rosemary, got all the fame. You still single?"

We chatted a while longer, then as I was about to say goodbye, I thought to ask, "What about a woman named Katy Bosun?"

"The dean's secretary? A good woman to have on your side, and a bad enemy. A major gossip."

"Was Carver the dean then?"

"Oh, no, just a professor. But the dean was retiring, and there was talk about Carver becoming dean. That's when I knew I had to get out."

"He's the one who hired me. I guess I'm not sexy, either, since he's never tried to touch me."

"Probably knows who your father is."

"One last name. Lowell Carragher. Owns a bookstore here in town."

"Buddy with David and Brett. Rich. You know he owns a lot more than that bookstore, right?"

"Yeah."

"Lowell's a strange one. Can't say anything negative about him, but I never really trusted him. I always got the feeling he considered the college as a play. Like a Shakespearean comedy staged for his entertainment."

With an occasional murder thrown in. I could see that.

※

The following Saturday, Steven drove in. He told me that he packed what he owned and truly cared about and shipped it to Wicklow, then packed his clothes and a few personal things into his sports car, and drove east. Everything else had gone to Goodwill.

"Are you hungry?" he asked. "I'll treat you to the Faculty Club."

"You're on."

We walked over, and I asked, "Did you talk to your buddy in Vegas about the Gambler Grimoire?"

"Yeah. I thought he'd bust a gut laughing. It's the unicorn of the gambling world."

"I knew that. Anyone offering it for sale or offering unrealistic amounts of money for it?"

"Both. You and I should write one. I think we can publish it on Amazon."

I glared at him.

"I'm serious, Savanna. My friend says you can buy one on about every corner in Las Vegas or Atlantic City. The only problem is finding one with spells that work."

"Yeah, that's the only problem I have with spells that turn lead into gold."

"If it was easy, everyone would be doing it."

Over dinner, I told him of my plan to try and scry Kavanaugh's murder.

"My specialty is more in the line of creating potions and poultices, not breaking and entering," Steven said. "I mean, it's locked, right?"

"Locks aren't a problem."

"Is that why you're a professor instead of a cat burglar? No challenge?"

"Something like that. I do need some help with the scrying spell, however. I'm not sure I can pull enough power for the spell."

Steven took a sip of his wine. "It does surprise me that no one thought of scrying the scene before. Maybe that's just not done with murders for some reason."

"No one I've met has accused Lieutenant Kagan of creativity or imagination."

After dinner, we went to the alchemy lab, gathered the tools we would need, then proceeded to Kavanaugh's apartment as the sun was setting. I sprang the lock, we entered, and set the equipment where it needed to be.

"He was killed by the fireplace?" Steven asked.

"Yes, and that's part of the puzzle," I replied. "The killer had to be between him and the fireplace to grab the poker." I walked over to where I had seen the blood spot before it was cleaned. "I get the impression his head was lying here when he was found."

"And where were his feet?"

"The chalk outline indicated here," I pointed.

"So, his body was lying parallel with the fireplace. What we don't know is where his assailant was standing."

"From what I was told, he was hit four times. Twice in the back of the head, once on the left side of the head, and once at the junction of his neck and shoulder on the right side. The tool stand was here, so I assume that is where the killer grabbed the poker from."

I began laying out the clear, soft plastic tubing filled with witch's salt. First, I laid the longest piece into a circle, then five straight pieces to create the pentagram inside.

"Interesting," Steven said. "I wouldn't have thought of that."

"I'm not going to be running a vacuum cleaner to clean up the salt," I said. "This is actually very handy anytime you're working in someone else's house. Someone who my father thought was a bad influence taught me about doing it."

The candle holders I set at the points of the pentagram were collapsible, as was the podium—actually, a sheet music stand—that I set in the middle of the pentagram. On one side of the podium, I set a piece of paper with the spell written out and held down by a small copper bowl, and on the other side, I set a six-inch glass lens.

"I have the spell memorized, so that is for you," I said.

Steven picked up the paper and read it, the second time silently mouthing the words.

"Okay, I think I've got it."

Little light came through the windows from the setting sun, and it was almost dark in the room. Drawing my wand, I touched each of the candles, lighting the wicks.

"Shall we begin?"

I recited the incantation alone the first time, letting Steven hear my cadence and intonation. He joined me as I began chanting the Latin words the second time. Halfway through the seventh recitation, the lens came to life.

Kavanaugh faced us. His mouth worked, but there was no sound. Since he was angry, and obviously shouting at times, it was difficult to read his lips. He turned away, and a fireplace poker appeared, sweeping down and striking him on the left side of his head.

Kavanaugh stumbled, and the poker descended again, and again, and again as he fell. A pool of blood began to spread, and the image in the lens faded.

"That's it? We don't get to see the killer?" There was outrage in Steven's voice.

"Sorry. I had Kavanaugh's DNA—I mean, it's all over the apartment—but since I don't know who the killer was, I couldn't give you the entire TV show. Did you notice the book lying on that table next to this chair? Not very thick, green with a red spine?"

"Yes, but I didn't try to read what it said. It looked like a journal or a ledger book."

"There wasn't any writing. But as far as I know, it wasn't removed by the police, and it wasn't here when I entered this place the first time. What else did you notice?"

"The killer was shorter than Kavanaugh was. You can tell by the angle of the blows. None of them came from above him."

I looked around. "Or the killer was sitting in that chair, grabbed the poker, and swung it before he or she stood up." I began gathering my tools and stuffing them in my duffle bag.

"Either way, I'm willing to bet the killer was a woman."

I chuckled. "You and everyone who knew him. How short would you guess? My height? Shorter? Taller?"

He considered. "Your height. The angle of the poker would be different if swung by someone very short."

"I agree. That eliminates one suspect." I blew out the last candle and put it in the bag. "Shall we go?"

CHAPTER 25

The major problems with teaching at a university of the arcane arts were the teachers and the students. Not only were they talented but also intelligent, and many were potentially dangerous. Witches had cast complex spells for centuries —most without any formal education—and underestimating anyone who might intend harm in a place such as Wicklow College was a serious mistake.

I was reminded of that as I walked past Kavanaugh's apartment the following morning. I didn't notice at first that I'd walked into a spider's trap. I proceeded four or five steps, each one meeting increasing resistance, before everything slowed down and my progress halted.

"You venture into dangerous territory," a bright sign read in front of me as I slowed. The sign slowly faded.

It had been many years since I concerned myself with surveillance and ambush. Either I was being watched, or someone had set a spell on Kavanaugh's rooms that sent an alert about my visit the night before. At least no one was trying to blow me up.

I took a deep breath, activated my wand, and shattered the

spell holding me. Unfortunately, that wouldn't send an intimidating message to anyone watching, as the spell hadn't been intended to hold me for long and was already fading.

It was a complex spell, or rather a set of spells. The sign was separate from the trap spell. The sign might be something a student picked up in a class, but the trap came from either a family grimoire or the Witches' Web. I couldn't imagine a legitimate reason for teaching it at Wicklow College.

Who else could I be putting in danger with my investigation? Steven, Kelly, and David had all been in Kavanaugh's apartment with me at various times. And Kagan, of course. Someone was concerned, and that was a cause for my concern. Someone had tried to kill me once already.

I walked through the quad, stopping by the coffee shop next to the Faculty Club before going to my first class. When I emerged, I noticed Emma and Ophelia standing together near the breezeway leading to Howard Quad. Were they watching me? As soon as I caught sight of them, they turned away and walked toward the classroom building on the other side of the quad.

<hr />

In my Introduction to Alchemy course that morning, a student asked, "How much of the science of alchemical magic is really documented and understood? I was reading a book from the library, and the author maintained that only half of what we consider magic is understood at all."

A different student asked, "What is the difference between religion and magic, or is there a difference?"

After escaping, I decided it might be a good idea to talk to someone who knew far more about magic than I did. There were a couple of my older friends in Sausalito who might have been able to shed some light on the Gambler Grimoire and other such books, but one of the grand experts on the history of magic was closer.

I walked outside the quads, found a bench under a large tree near the library, and made my call.

"Dad? Have you got some time? I have a problem."

"I always have time for you, sweetheart. What's going on?"

It took almost forty minutes—occasionally interrupted by my father's questions—to tell him the whole story.

"Okay. So, other than telling you that you should move somewhere safer," he said, "or be sensible and leave this thing alone, what do you need from me?"

I sighed. "I keep getting the feeling that this book, or at least the spirit of this book, is something that captures people. That I can't really leave it alone, and that people will continue to die until the book is locked away someplace safe. Does that make any sense, or am I just being obsessive and paranoid?"

"I doubt that the spirit of the book is influencing people who've never seen or held it," he said. "But the idea—the concept—of the book seems to have taken hold of some people's imaginations. Assuming you're right, and all these deaths are connected—and connected to the book—then I would say finding the book is almost like a religious quest. I agree with you that it's more than the idea of riches. The possibility of changing the future, of loading the dice for things far beyond simply games of chance, could mean something very different to different people. It could have very different ramifications, depending on what people wanted to do with it, or the ways they might conceive of using it."

"You don't think I'm crazy?"

"Not any more than I did before you called. Anything else you need from me?"

"Yes, I need you to check on some people for me." I gave him several names, then hung up.

My next call was to Kagan.

"Lieutenant? Savanna Robinson."

"Don't tell me you found another body."

I bit my tongue, then continued when I managed not to laugh. "No, I just thought I should tell you that someone is harassing me. Some men with British accents confronted me in town the other day. They seem to think I know something about that GG book. And then today, I had something odd happen on campus."

"Odd?"

"I'm not sure how much I should say over the phone."

"Ahh. I see. Are you free this afternoon?"

"I will be, after three-thirty."

"I'll stop by."

"Thank you, Lieutenant. One thing I was curious about. You didn't find any women's hair in Kavanaugh's apartment, did you?"

The guffaw from Kagan confirmed my guess. "Take your pick—blonde, brunette, or redhead. We've ruled out the redhead."

"Really?"

"She was serving me a beer at Shillelagh at the time he was killed."

"Only one?"

"Yes, only one beer. And only one redhead—natural redhead. They are a very small minority of the population, you know."

"Thank you, Lieutenant. I'll see you this afternoon."

When Kagan came, I served tea and banana bread I'd baked. As I suspected from his shape, Kagan liked to eat.

I told him first about the spider trap and the message that

morning, not mentioning my foray with Steven into Kavanaugh's apartment. Then I told him about being accosted in town.

"Lowell Carragher said the man's name is George Peterson. Remember the correspondence we found between Kavanaugh and Harold Merriweather in London? This Peterson character showed up at Merriweather's shop a couple of weeks ago. That night, the shop was burglarized, and Merriweather's copy of that correspondence was taken. Then Peterson shows up here."

The sour expression on Kagan's face told me that he wished the whole Kavanaugh mess would go away, and take me with it.

"You didn't happen to identify any of the DNA at Kavanaugh's—other than the redhead's—did you?" I asked.

Kagan shook his head. "I can't go around asking every woman in town for a DNA sample. The only reason I know about the redhead is that she volunteered that she'd spent the night with him a few days before he was killed. She's a friend I went to high school with, and she didn't want me to think she was trying to hide something. They seem to have had an informal arrangement—nothing serious—and her boss told me they had been meeting for years."

He sighed. "Dr. Robinson, we found hair samples from seven different women—four of them in his bed. It made me wonder how often he changed his sheets, but it does lend some credence to the theory that he was killed by a jealous lover."

CHAPTER 26

"Dr. Robinson?"

Ophelia trotted toward me on Howard Quad while I was on my way to the Faculty Club to meet Kelly for dinner.

"Hi, what's up?" I asked, giving the girl a smile.

She slowed and fell in beside me. "I just wanted to tell you, they let Corey out on bail. I kept telling them that Josh attacked Corey, and the knife they found was Josh's."

"That's good to hear, I guess. It still doesn't change the fact that a young man is dead."

The girl's face fell. "That's true. What a mess. I wish it had never happened."

I shook my head. "Three deaths of people you knew fairly well. It's been a rough year."

Ophelia nodded. "It really has. I mean, this is the sort of thing you read about. The sort of thing that happens to other people."

"Make you sort of wish you'd gone to school in Boulder?"

"Who said anything about Boulder?"

"I heard you were accepted there."

"Yeah, but I never really considered it. It was my backup if I didn't make it here at Wicklow. Dr. Aubert wasn't very supportive, but Dr. Kavanaugh offered me the job at the greenhouse and agreed to be my advisor."

"If you don't mind my asking, what was Dr. Aubert's issue?"

"He wanted me to do my thesis in protective amulets, which is his area of study. As I told you, I want to do potions."

I leaned down. "Sometimes professors get a little grabby with students' ideas, don't they?"

Ophelia turned wide, frightened eyes toward me.

I winked. "A roommate of mine had a professor publish a paper she wrote. It happens."

"I've heard of things like that."

"I have to go," I said, "but you keep your head down. There's some strange stuff going on around here, and you and Corey don't want to get caught up in any more of it."

"Yes, ma'am. My lawyer says that we're not out of the woods yet."

I watched her trudge toward the graduate student dorm where she and Emma lived. And probably Corey, but I hadn't bothered to find out about that. I continued to the Faculty Club.

Kelly had already showed up and grabbed a table by the only window in the room, giving us a view out on the quad.

"Does it give you an eerie feeling to walk past where that kid was killed?" Kelly asked as I sat down. "It kind of does me, and I didn't even see the body. It really weirds me out when I pass by Agnes's shop."

"But not Brett Kavanaugh's apartment?"

"To an extent, but that's three floors up, and it's been six months."

Leaning closer over the table, inviting Kelly also to lean closer, I said, "I have some new info from Kagan. He told me they collected hair samples from seven women in Kavanaugh's apartment, including four from his bed."

Kelly grinned and shook her head. "Doesn't surprise me. I wonder if any of them knew about the others."

"I wondered if any of them were there at the same time," I said, and we laughed.

"That's something I hadn't considered," Kelly said. "Maybe more than one person killed him."

We were speaking in low tones, but I dropped my voice even lower. "That is something I considered with Agnes. Tell me, you've got books of power in the museum, right?"

"Some. Some are on display, some are locked away in the Archives, and some are locked away in an alchemist's safe in the Archives."

"Suppose I had a book that looked rather ordinary—like a journal or a ledger book I could buy at any store. And I copied a bunch of rare spells into it. Would it feel like a book of power?"

The waitress showed up and took our order. After she went away, Kelly said, "It depends a lot on how the spells were copied. Simply copying the words wouldn't necessarily help anyone cast the spells. Why?"

"I cast a scrying spell. I'm not very good at it, and don't have a lot of power for that sort of thing, but I think Kavanaugh had a book—green with a red spine that looked like a journal you'd buy in a stationary store. Nothing fancy, and not old. We didn't find anything like that in either his apartment or his office."

Kelly took a sip of her wine. "You do know how to copy a spell, right? The words are only part of it. To make sure someone else can cast it, you have to pronounce the words as they're written, with the proper pronunciation, including intonation, inflection, rhythm, etcetera."

"Yes. I have my dad's grimoire, and occasionally he'll ask me to send him a spell from it. I'm glad I didn't have to wait for him to die before I could use it, so that's the accommodation I make for him."

"Right. So, depending on how the spells were written, it makes a difference as to whether the book has any power or any use."

"So, there could be dozens of Gambler Grimoires floating around, some worthless, some extraordinarily powerful," I said.

"Exactly. Like that *Maleficium Spiritus* we found. That was the real thing, but someone could copy spells from it that would be worthless."

"I can feel magic in artifacts and books and things," I said. "But you have a special talent for it, right?"

Kelly nodded. "I'm a librarian. It's a talent I was born with. Uncle Harold recognized it when I was very young, and I was given special training, just as you were with alchemy. Dr. Phillips has it. Brett didn't. The chance to study under Dr. Phillips was the original reason I came to Wicklow."

"Would you recognize it in someone?"

"I don't know. I think Edmund might. Partly, I can pick up on it because of something a person can do, like untie knotted spells, or see through certain kinds of illusions, or read spells that are beyond my power to cast."

It took a minute for me to digest that last part, since it contradicted something I'd been taught since my magic first manifested. "You're saying that if I gave you my grimoire, you could read the healing spells, or the master alchemy spells, even though you have no healing talent or alchemy talent?"

"Yes, although the supposition about my alchemy talent is sort of off base. Edmund believes—and a fair number of librarians and alchemists agree with him—that the librarian talent contains a sort of mutation of alchemy. I can create and unlock an alchemist's safe, for instance. I can ward or unward, and shield charms, amulets, and other kinds of artifacts."

"Can you make a wand?"

Kelly shook her head. "No, but I can ward one, make it useless."

"Sort of a null-magic spell?"

"No. Once I remove the ward, the wand would still work. The spell just disconnects it from magic. It's complex, and not a quick and easy spell."

"You don't know anyone who is a forensic witch, do you? Someone who could use a strand of hair to scry who the hair belongs to?"

"Nope, but you could talk to Dr. Evans at the infirmary, or the medical examiner with the county, Dr. Parsons. And speaking of wands, the wand I have was a gift from Uncle Harold when I graduated college. Is it one of yours?"

I had seen her wand that night in Kavanaugh's apartment, and it definitely wasn't something I had crafted. "No. I'm pretty sure it's from Gerard Toussaint, a wandsmith in Lyon, France. Harold handled a lot of his wands. I never made that many, but last year I started trying to put some money away so I could get out of San Francisco. I'm a little slow sometimes, but I finally figured out that the Institute in Sausalito was going to string me along forever without giving me a full-time position. That's how I could lure Steven here. He was in the same boat."

"Mom said she would send a check for the wands. It sort of seems like a lot of money."

I nodded. "They take a lot of time to make, and the materials I use are expensive and difficult to find. That's why I sold them through Merriweather's instead of on the street corner. I'll have to find another outlet for them now."

CHAPTER 27

"Katy, is there a travel agency here in town?" I asked. "Or does everyone just make arrangements on the internet?"

She looked up from the computer, where she was typing something. "You can do it on the internet if you wish, but I book most of the travel for faculty and upper-level administrative staff. If it's something like a conference that you want the college to pay for, then you need to do it through me. Why, where do you need to go?"

"I was just wondering about Dr. Kavanaugh and where he went last Christmas. I ran across some papers I gave to Lieutenant Kagan—correspondence with a bookseller in England."

"That's where he went. He and Kelly flew out of Pittsburgh right after the end of the term. Went to DC, then on to London."

"Dr. Kavanaugh and Kelly?"

"Dr. Robinson, you can't imagine what it's like trying to book flights out of Pittsburgh for the holidays. There are at least a dozen colleges and universities in the area that let out about the same time. But I remember their bookings specifically because Brett and Kelly wanted to get out a day earlier than everyone else, and they flew back from London on New Year's Day."

I was used to making my own travel arrangements, and I made a note to myself that if I wanted to keep anything private, not to tell Katy about it.

"You wouldn't happen to know a redhead that Dr. Kavanaugh was dating, would you?" I asked.

Katy rolled her eyes. "Seanan Murphy. She's a cousin of mine. I wouldn't consider it dating. I think more like a booty call. She's a bartender down at Shillelagh. Her father owns the place, but he's retired. You'd think both of them would know better. She was still in high school when Brett knocked her up. Paid her family a goodly bit of change to hush it up. It would have been his job if they'd a made a stink. But the two of them could never keep their hands off each other."

"And he was how old?"

"In his thirties."

"Did he make a habit of that sort of thing?"

Katy shrugged. "It wasn't the first time. Personally, I would have looked at Seanan first thing when he was killed, but I think Sam Kagan is sweet on her."

"Did she keep the baby?"

"Oh, yeah. Brett paid child support, but Seanan could never get him to marry her. Why buy the cow when milk is free?"

"It doesn't sound like the milk was free."

"Not as expensive as a wife would have been." Katy chuckled and winked at me. "You know how women are. She would have wanted a house, a car, nice clothes. And he'd have to take her to functions here at the college. The girl's sweet, and good-looking, but dumb as a hammer. Brett would have been embarrassed."

That evening, I talked Steven into driving me into town, and we went to dinner at Shillelagh.

As far as American Irish pubs went, it was an American Irish pub. The menu was what I expected, including corned beef and cabbage, cottage pie, and fish and chips. There were few beer taps—Guinness, Smithwick's, and Harp—and American beers were available in bottles. The food was good, and there was plenty of it.

The bartender and two of the waitresses were redheads, and there was a strong family resemblance.

When our waitress came to clear the dishes, I asked with a laugh, "Do you have to have red hair to work here?"

"Family operation," the waitress said. "My momma didn't have any brown-haired kids."

After the waitress left, I saw that Steven was smirking at me.

"What?"

"That's my question. What was that about? I didn't realize you were fond of Irish pub grub or redheaded Irish girls."

"According to the gossip, Brett Kavanaugh and the bartender were buddies. Even had a kid together."

"Ahh. I sure hope you catch his killer soon."

"I hope his killer is caught before I get murdered, too. I don't care who does the catching."

"Keep your nose out of other people's business, and there'll be less chance someone wants to blow it off."

I glared at him. "Bombs and poisons are cowardly weapons."

"Says the girl with enough power to melt someone's brain in their skull."

"Shhh. That's not even true. Do you see those women who just came in and sat at the bar? The ones talking to the bartender? The one with light-brown hair in a braid is Iris

Bishop. Her sister Agnes used to work in your greenhouse and was murdered. The other woman is Helen Donnelly, your predecessor as horticultural manager."

"Do you know that my high school had more people than there are in this town?"

"Mine, too. It will help you broaden your horizons."

"Or narrow them."

"No one in Wicklow is going to try and burn you at the stake."

"True. Not for being a witch, anyway. No gay bars."

"No over-forty dance bars, either. But no one in San Francisco or New York or Paris offered me a job."

"And I wasn't born king. The world isn't fair."

※

It was late when I got in, but the call from my father didn't surprise me. For the past twenty years, I had lived one time zone earlier than he did, and now I was two time zones later. It would take a while for him to get used to it.

"Hi, Dad. What's up?"

"Got some information on some of those names you asked about."

"Great!"

"Agnes and Iris Bishop. You do know that the Bishop name in Salem goes back to the time the town was settled, right? Prominently mentioned in the witch trials. Family seems to have fallen on hard times. Nothing unusual pops up, though. Rebecca Hall. She works for me here in Santa Fe, you know? I sponsored her daughter to pharmacy school in Albuquerque."

"What do you know about the girl's father?"

"Professor at Wicklow up until his death last spring, if that's what you mean. That's where Rebecca is from."

"So, you know Emma?"

"For most of her life."

"Thanks, Dad."

Surely, Emma must have known who I was. Why hadn't she ever said anything, even when I talked about using Seth Robinson as a resource for Emma's dissertation research?

CHAPTER 28

The email-form letter from the computer lab was innocuous but got my attention.

Please provide, for each personal computer you own:
 Make
 Model
Serial Number
Hard drive size
Amount of memory
Any specialized software installed by Wicklow College

I picked up my office phone and called Kelly. "Hey, why do you need all this information on my personal computer?"

"Standard security procedure. Cuts down on theft, makes it easier to identify and recover computers that do get stolen."

"Is this for all students, faculty, and staff?"

"Yes. Why?"

"And if you find a computer that isn't registered with you?"

"Then we register it."

"How do you know if it's registered or not?"

"It's in our database, and I give you a sticker to put on your machine." Kelly sounded a little irked. "It's really not a big deal, Savanna."

"How many computers in your active database match the fancy new machine Brett Kavanaugh bought himself last Christmas?"

A few moments of silence, then, "Three computers of that brand and model. And one has the same serial number as Brett's, which shouldn't be possible."

"Anyone we know?"

"Ophelia Harkness."

"Do you still have the information on Agnes Bishop's computer in your system?"

"Yeah. Hang on a minute."

More silence.

"Savanna, I should call Sam Kagan. I've got some strange things here that I shouldn't have."

"Lunch?"

"Yeah. I'll call you if I can't make it."

I was deciding between the two lunch specials or one of my favorites from the menu when Kelly sat down across from me.

"So? What happened?" I asked.

Kelly shook her head. "I'm not sure Sam Kagan should be running a murder investigation, let alone three. I remember you kept asking about computers and grimoires, but no one ever asked who worked in computer operations here on campus."

"And?"

"Both Josh Tupper and Corey Lindsay worked in the computer lab, which is where we maintain the inventory database. There's a known bug in the system that allows duplicates. Oh, it flags the duplicate, but all you have to do is mark it as obsolete, and it sort of hides it from most searches. Usually that means the computer died, or was sold, or the owner left Wicklow. We do a mass update at the end of each term. A lot of buying and selling between students goes on."

"You didn't know they worked for you?"

I was rewarded with a glower. "I don't micromanage. Ted hires students who are computer savvy, and I trust him to keep them honest."

We ordered lunch, then Kelly continued. "Ophelia sold her computer to another student, and Corey entered Brett's in as her new machine. But here's the big thing—Agnes's missing computer is registered to Corey, and so is Josh's."

"What happens now?"

"Kagan arrested Ophelia and Corey again."

"You're a woman of many talents," I said.

Kelly shrugged. "A master of library science nowadays requires a bit more than memorizing the Dewey Decimal system. It is essentially a computer systems degree. There are three systems administrators on campus—a guy who handles the business computer systems, a guy who handles facilities, and me, who handles the library and academic computing services. Facilities have a subsystem that runs food services and inventory."

I had kept asking about Kavanaugh's computer because of the correspondence between him and Merriweather. It might also contain research he had done on the GG book. People died, their computers disappeared, and no one seemed concerned. I wondered if Kagan knew how to use a computer.

Upon returning to my office, I called Kagan.

"I hear you recovered computers belonging to Brett Kavanaugh and Agnes Bishop."

"Possibly."

"I talked to Kelly. While you're snooping around, look for a thin green book with a red spine. I think that's the motive for everything. I'll bet its contents are handwritten, not printed."

"I'll keep an eye out for it," Kagan said. "You know both of them have bailed out already. Their lawyers got to the jail about the same time I got there with the kids."

"Bail? For murder?"

"I couldn't arrest them for murder, though that might still happen. Possession of stolen property. But I am on my way to serve search warrants. Josh Tupper's computer is still missing."

"I don't suppose there's a chance I could get a couple of hours with Kavanaugh's computer?" I asked.

"A snowball's chance in hell. An expert with the State Police is on his way to take possession of it."

"Is he a witch? I'd be careful with what you let someone from outside dig around."

Kagan paused, then said, "The only computer expert witch I know is Kelly Grace, and since she's a potential suspect in Kavanaugh's murder, that's a problem."

I thought for a moment. "I know someone on the Council. Can you hold the State Police expert for a day?"

"Sure. Tomorrow's Friday, I'll just tell him to wait until next week. I doubt I'll get an argument."

Immediately after Sam hung up the phone, I dialed my father and explained the situation.

"I'm sure there is someone on the Pennsylvania State Police with the proper qualifications," he said. "Let me work on it."

He called back two hours later. "I found your man. Give me the phone number of the local cop who's working the case."

Kagan called an hour later. "I'm impressed. State headquarters in Harrisburg just called and said they are sending a different forensic computer expert out to help me with the case. Then he gave me a call to tell me he's a witch."

"Well, I'm glad it worked out. If there really is a Gambler Grimoire, it would be nice to try and find it."

"Do you know if Merriweather's computer in London was stolen?" Kagan asked.

Remembering Harold, I had to smile. "No computer, Lieutenant. He didn't believe in them."

I didn't have classes on Fridays, just a tutorial with my graduate students in the Apothecary lab in the late morning. I had just taken fresh pumpkin bread from the oven and brewed a pot of tea when there was a knock on my door.

The man standing there was tall, broad-shouldered, and extraordinarily good-looking.

"Dr. Robinson?"

"Yes?"

"I'm Lieutenant James Barclay with State Police computer forensics. Do you have a few minutes?"

"Certainly. Come in, Lieutenant." I saw his nostrils dilate. "I just pulled some pumpkin bread out of the oven. Would you care for a slice and some tea?"

"That smells great."

I led him to the kitchen and served him and myself a slice of the bread, placed butter and the teapot on the table, and sat across from him. I figured him for mid-to-early forties, and I was very aware of his eyes following me around the kitchen.

"What can I do for you, Lieutenant?"

"I understand that you're the reason I'm here. You're Seth Robinson's daughter?"

"I am. But the problem is a book—purported to be a specialized grimoire—four murders, and several missing computers. Lieutenant Kagan arranged for a computer expert from Pittsburgh to come out and look at a couple of computers that were recovered, but the expert isn't a witch. Considering the possibility that the murders may deal with a grimoire, and that all the victims and suspects are witches..."

He nodded. "I see the problem. The locals should have seen it as well."

"I got the feeling that they don't have a list of arcane coppers hanging on the wall."

Barclay raised his eyebrows. "Chief Crumley should. I'll suggest it to him. This bread is very good."

"It's autumn, and the pumpkins are ripe. Someone gave me one, and I really don't care for pumpkin pie, so I find other ways of using it."

"I did some checking before I came out here from Harrisburg," he said. "You used to work for the Council?"

I shook my head. "Twenty years ago. I worked as a sort of jack-of-all-trades investigator when I first graduated college and didn't know what I wanted to do with my life. Got to travel, see the world, and meet a lot of very interesting people."

We talked for about an hour. I laid out my reasoning and suspicions, then Barclay left, and I got ready for my tutorial.

I had to admit, the lingering up-and-down look he gave me before I shut the door made me feel pretty good. He wasn't wearing a wedding ring, either.

CHAPTER 29

Both Emma and Lia were absent from the tutorial. Emma's absence was strange, as she was always punctual and had never missed a session or an appointment.

When the tutorial was over, and the students finished cleaning up and had left, I lingered a while, checking the inventory of herbs and other items I would need for my labs the following week.

It was about twenty after twelve when I left the lab. The nights were getting cold enough that the plants in the outdoor herb garden were affected. Steven and his staff had harvested many of the plants and transplanted some into the greenhouse. Rather than go to my apartment, I turned toward the greenhouse to check on the available quantities of a few herbs I was going to need.

I was almost to the door when I heard a muffled scream from inside. Rushing through the airlock into the greenhouse, I saw Emma. The young woman was standing in the main aisle, looking toward the far end.

And the sight of what was there stopped me in my tracks. The cat, Koshka, trotted toward me, mewling pitifully. Whipping my wand out, I swung it in a slashing motion. "*Incisio!*" Reaching down, I caught up the cat with my other hand and hugged her to me. She buried her head in my armpit, making distressed noises.

The woman hanging from the greenhouse frame fell to the ground. I raced past Emma, but as I approached the girl on the ground, I realized there was no hurry. Ophelia was dead. I put the back of my hand against her cheek. Her skin was too cool.

"Lieutenant Kagan?" I said after setting the cat down and dialing my phone with shaking hands. "Can you come to the campus greenhouse? Ophelia Harkness is dead."

I called the campus police, then leaned back against one of the growing benches, and stared at Lia. She had been hung using parachute cord, which was used to string shade cloth in some parts of the herb garden during the hottest summer weather. She was wearing a red shirt, blue jeans, and sneakers.

After carefully scrutinizing the area around the body, I turned toward Emma, who had followed me to that end of the greenhouse. Although Emma's face was pale, she didn't seem as upset as I felt.

"I missed you two for our tutorial," I said. "I think I know why Lia didn't show up, what about you?"

"I-I-uh-she—" Emma stammered.

"What were you doing in here?"

"I-I was looking for Lia."

Over Emma's shoulder, I saw Steven come into the greenhouse and walk toward us.

"So, you weren't with her earlier this morning?" I asked Emma.

"Uh, no. She went someplace after breakfast."

"She was in the lab earlier," Steven said. Emma jumped and whirled around. "I thought I saw you in the lab, too." His brow furrowed in question.

"Uh, I just stopped in for a moment, but I didn't see her."

"That must have been early," I said. "I was in there from about twenty to ten until I heard you scream."

"I-I came in and saw her."

Lia's body was blocked from Steven's sight by the two of us standing between him and the dead girl. He moved to the side a little, and I saw his eyes widen, then shift to my face.

"She's dead," I said. "Can you go to the Apothecary lab and make sure no one goes in there? I think the police will want to check things over. Don't touch anything."

"Yeah, I'll do that," Steven said. "You've called them?"

"Uh-huh. I expect they'll show up pretty quickly."

The campus police did show up just as Steven was leaving. They spoke with him for a couple of minutes, then he left with one of them, and the other policeman walked to where Emma and I were standing.

"Ophelia Harkness," I said. "Graduate student. She worked here in the greenhouse."

Dr. Evans from the campus infirmary came in shortly after, then Lieutenants Kagan and Barclay came a few minutes later.

I gave my statement to Kagan while Barclay spoke with Emma. When I was finished, Dr. Evans motioned me over to the body. I gave Kagan a questioning look, and he handed me gloves and shoe covers.

"What is the smell on her breath?" Evans asked.

I bent over, inhaled deeply, then stood up. "Something I might give someone if I planned to kill them and wanted them compliant." I turned to Kagan. "You might look for a small bottle. She's taken some sort of tincture. Something to knock her out, I think."

Turning my attention back to Evans, I said, "I smell a mixture of stuff. The smells I can readily identify include St. John's wort, valerian, and kava kava. Maybe using pure ethanol as the reagent, but more likely vodka. Smells pretty strong, which would take it beyond the therapeutic dosages. I still wouldn't put all three of those things together. I can't tell from smell, but I'll bet it was magically enhanced."

"How did you cut her down without touching her?" Kagan asked.

"Magic. Do you see what she stood on?"

"I think that bench where those plants are moved aside." He pointed to several potted plants that had been pushed away from the edge of the bench next to Lia's body.

"That would work for the final act. What was used to tie the cord to the frame up there? I couldn't reach the roof from that bench and I'm a good half-a-foot taller than she was."

Kagan looked around, spotted an eight-foot stepladder leaning against the wall fifty feet away.

"That, maybe."

"Nice of whoever tied the rope to put the ladder away for us. Someone could trip over it and get hurt."

Kagan glared at me. Barclay rolled his eyes and turned away. Emma suddenly looked more frightened than she had before. Evans looked around at everyone, rather speculatively, from my point of view.

Looking down at Lia's blue face, I felt like I wanted to throw up. I was so sorry for her. The fear and the panic she had shown when we last spoke weighed on me. Then another thought struck me.

"Dr. Evans," I said, "I think we should consider her only provisionally dead."

"And what the hell does that mean?" Kagan asked.

I watched Emma's face as I said, "There are drugs that, in the proper dosages, mimic death. Depending on how long she hung, whether or not her neck is broken, there is a possibility she could recover."

"What kind of drug?" Evans asked.

"Tetrodotoxin—an extract from puffer fish—is one possibility. It's used in the first step for the creation of a voodoo zombie. I don't know if we have any of it in our inventories, but Dr. McCallum and I can check."

"You're saying that you don't think this is a suicide," Lieutenant Barclay said.

"I'm saying that if it is, she went to a lot of trouble to complicate it." I turned to Emma. "You were looking for her. Why? Was there something you were concerned about?"

"She was kinda depressed, and she didn't show up to study with me like we planned. We were going to go over our notes before your tutorial."

Emma acted as though she was fishing for words. "I mean, it's been rough on her lately. She keeps getting arrested, and no one has really accused her of doing anything. She told me she was afraid she'd get sent to prison, her whole life ruined, just because two guys got in a fight."

Eventually, Ophelia's body was taken to the college infirmary rather than the city morgue. The police told me I could go, but as I was leaving the greenhouse, Dr. Evans pulled me aside.

"What is that puffer fish BS you were telling the cops? You don't really believe that girl is still alive, do you?"

"No, nor do I believe that she mixed and took a cocktail of botanicals that would knock her out, and then went clambering around with ladders and ropes and all that to hang herself."

Evans nodded. "I've had enough apothecary courses to understand the drugs you mentioned, and I agree with you."

"Unless they find the vial the tincture was in here, then it would mean she took it at her dorm or some other place, managed to walk all the way over here, mess with that ladder, tie knots, and all that. If what she took was as strong as I think it was, she'd have been more likely to die of a broken neck falling off that ladder. Doctor, she was doing research in potions, and she was smart. I don't buy that she drugged herself, then hung herself. She could have painlessly poisoned herself without all the fuss."

CHAPTER 30

Bad news, of course, travels quickly. Salacious news travels faster. In less than half an hour, I was at the Faculty Club with Steven, Kelly, and David. At least I had to repeat my story only once.

"I'm sure the girl was upset," I said after I finished, "but when I talked to her last, she was scared, and exasperated that Kagan was targeting her. Tupper's death was a minor inconvenience in her mind. She just wanted it all to be over so she could go back to her life."

"She didn't consider accessory and obstruction a big deal?" David said.

"No, not really. She basically said that Kagan was an idiot for expecting her to tattle on her boyfriend. David, you've been here a lot longer than I have. How entitled do all these rich kids see themselves? And you all should know, kids consider adults the enemy in many ways."

Steven nodded. "Their societal norms and adult societal norms are two circles that don't completely overlap. Even when they understand what society's laws, morals, and ethics are, and the reasons behind them, it doesn't mean such things apply to them personally."

"Exactly. I had to remind her that no matter what else was going on, Joshua Tupper is dead. Yes, I understand that she didn't immediately call the cops to report it, but she couldn't expect everyone to ignore it. It just turns my stomach that someone killed her, though."

"But if you're right, and she was murdered," David said, "who is your suspect? Corey? I mean, with her dead, there's no witness to Tupper's killing."

I shook my head. "He's basically confessed, but says it was self-defense. And they have enough evidence that they don't need her statements. In fact, he's just lost the only witness in his favor. I think it goes back to the recovery of Kavanaugh's computer and that damned book."

"The mythical grimoire," David said.

"Yes, but I'm starting to think that wasn't the reason Kavanaugh was killed." I considered telling them my suspicions, but it really wasn't fair since I had no proof.

"Back to the jealous lover theory?" Kelly asked.

"Jilted woman," I said. "I'm beginning to think the book was stolen by someone other than his killer."

"Who do you think knew he had it?" David asked.

"I think Lowell Carragher knew, or at least suspected, and I'm beginning to think Agnes, Helen, Ophelia, and Emma knew. I think he bragged. Emma and Lia told me about some major arguments he had with Agnes and Helen just before he died."

"If that's the case," Kelly said, "then Helen or Emma would be the logical choices for who has it."

"As well as the logical choices for who killed Ophelia," Steven said.

"And the next logical targets for our English grimoire hunters," I said. "One thing for certain, if it falls into my hands,

I'm dumping it on someone else like a hot potato. The damned thing's cursed, whether it's real or not."

To my mind, Ophelia's killing took the whole mess at Wicklow up another notch. Either she had the grimoire and someone killed her for it, or someone thought the girl knew too much about at least one of the other murders. A third possibility could have been blackmail.

Ophelia's ethics were a little too loose for me. I knew that rich kids were used to their parents buying their way out of trouble. I was all too familiar with their feelings of invulnerability. Some of the spells they attempted every semester always left me shaking my head in disbelief.

The girl's murder seemed to place the killer on campus, but I wanted to be sure. There were two people off campus I needed to talk to.

The bus let me off a block from Lowell Carragher's bookstore. As far as I could tell, none of Peterson's London crowd were standing around watching either the bus stop or the store, but who knew what spells they might have sprinkled about.

"Well, it is my lucky day!" Lowell said when I walked into the shop.

"Not necessarily. Wicklow's on a roll that would make Agatha Christie blush. Another murder at the college."

"And of course, the first thing you thought of was to come here and accuse me of it." His grin and a wink let me know he was joking.

"I'm not the accusatory sort," I said. "Did you sneak onto campus earlier today and murder a coed? Steal her grimoire? Plant pot seeds in her apothecary project? Enquiring minds want to know."

He chortled. "You make it sound like fun. Instead, I've been here trying to figure out why in the world this terrible book has been nominated for a Pulitzer Prize." He held up a copy of a best seller I had seen the author parade through all the TV shows before I arrived at Wicklow College and discovered television no longer existed.

"Okay, then have you fenced a copy of the Gambler Grimoire this afternoon?"

"Just a moment, let me check. I've been so busy with people attempting to sell me mythical artifacts, I haven't had time to see what exactly I spent my money on."

He took a deep breath, and his face took on a more serious expression. "Seriously? Another murder? Anyone I know?"

I shook my head. "I sort of doubt it. A graduate student named Ophelia Harkness. She was found hanged in the greenhouse."

He studied my face. "Not suicide?"

"I doubt it."

"You know, I checked up on you."

"It seems a number of people are entertaining themselves that way. Not hard to do. I'm using my real name."

"I noticed. Whereas most people I know spent their youth partying and traveling, you worked as an investigator for the Witches' Council."

"I was always a creative child. Why misspend my youth in a conventional way? Besides, the Council paid for me to travel and party. A mutually beneficial arrangement, although they tended to send me to places I wouldn't have frequented if left to my own inclinations. How well do you know Helen Donnelly?"

"Well enough. We dated in our early twenties. Good apothecary, decent alchemist. Very good accountant. Why?"

"In the days prior to his death, Brett Kavanaugh had a couple of major rows with Agnes Bishop and Helen Donnelly. I'm wondering if the arguments might have had something to do with the Gambler Grimoire. And is there a woman in this town you haven't dated?"

Lowell cocked his head to the side, and his face assumed a thoughtful expression. "I could see Agnes reacting to such magic. Rather a puritan, in some ways. Truly someone who thought of magic as a religion, and a devotee of the Earth Goddess. Helen, no. Any fights she had with Brett were probably over his love life, and the fact she wasn't in it. She never got over him."

"Did you know that he had a purported copy of that grimoire?"

He shook his head. "I knew that he went to London to look at it, but if he brought it back, he didn't tell me."

"I wondered if he bragged about it. Was he prone to do such a thing? Especially to women?"

"Possibly. The fancy car, flashy clothes, holidays in exotic locations. He thought such things impressed women."

"Such things do impress some women. We found some very impressive books in his collection, for the magical literary sort of girl."

"Really? I'd be willing to take a look at them. Give you an estimate of the market values."

"Black magic grimoires? The Council takes a dim view of selling such things. If the college museum doesn't want them, I'll probably talk to my father. I'm not sure I trust anyone to play with them. Since I gave up becoming queen, I've been a little picky concerning who wields world-changing spells."

His surprise didn't seem faked. "Oh really? No, I've managed to sail beneath the Council's notice for fifty-two years. I think I'll leave that particular thrill for someone younger and dumber."

"You didn't know that Brett dabbled in such collectables?"

Lowell shook his head. "A few questionable artifacts, but no, not dark magic books. And he didn't get them through me."

"*Malificium Spiritus*," I said. "Kelly says it's the real thing."

He shuddered. "People dabble in things they don't understand, then act shocked when they get burned."

"That's how I feel about the Gambler Grimoire. Even if it's fake, people are getting killed over it."

CHAPTER 31

Lowell informed me that a bus ran by Helen's nursery only twice a day—early in the morning going west, and again at suppertime going east. Its major purpose was to convey commuters to the west bank and back for the nursery and a couple of other businesses. I figured I could talk Steven into running me out there.

That evening after dinner, there was a knock on my front door. I checked the scrying lens I had set up, and saw a tall young man nervously fidgeting. Corey Lindsay.

Considering my suspicions and his admitted behavior, I took my wand in my left hand and held it in the folds of my skirt before opening the door.

"Yes?"

"Professor Robinson? I'm Corey Lindsay. I need to talk to you."

I ushered him in, and he ducked through the door. We sat in front of the fireplace. We had actually never met before. I had seen him only at a distance. A good-looking kid, sandy hair, lean, and well over six feet tall.

"Lia didn't kill herself," he said.

"I don't think she did, either. Who do you think had a reason to do that?"

"Maybe Agnes's sister."

"And why would she? I mean, did she even know Lia?"

"Or Emma."

"Again, why? Corey, you're going to have to tell me a lot more to convince me. Simply throwing wild accusations around isn't very helpful. You might as well tell me that Joshua's ghost did it."

"Yeah. We did some stupid stuff, though."

"I have, too, although I never killed anyone. Do you have a book? Something that might be called a Gambler Grimoire?"

He had been sitting with his elbows on his knees, head down, but that caused him to jerk, his eyes on my face.

"How did you know about that?" He shook his head. "Lia had it. I don't know if it's still in her room, or if she hid it somewhere else."

"You don't think that was the reason she was killed? Where did she get it?"

"I dunno."

"Don't know where she got it, or don't know why she was killed? Besides Helen and Emma, who else knows about the book?"

I could tell that he wanted me to buy into his story but didn't want to tell me some of it.

"Did you and Lia kill Agnes Bishop?" I asked.

Once again, his eyes snapped to my face, only this time his face showed fear. I leaned back in my chair and waited, my wand still in my left hand, hanging down to the side of my chair out of his sight.

"She attacked me. Us."

My first reaction was that a number of people had attacked him, and then ended up dead. The story came out, gradually, in bits and pieces. Kavanaugh had bragged about the grimoire, and Agnes let it be known that in her mind, the kind of magic that it represented was a perversion of the natural order. She and Kavanaugh argued, and then Helen joined in on Agnes's side. According to Corey, the back-and-forth sniping went on for weeks, then blew up into the shouting match Emma told me about the day Kavanaugh was killed.

According to Corey—and he admitted that a lot of what he told me was second or thirdhand—Emma and Kavanaugh were having an affair. Evidently on the night he was killed, Emma was at his apartment, and Lia saw her leave in the late evening. As soon as she did, Agnes appeared from the direction of the parking lot and went up to the apartment. Shortly thereafter, she came back down, got in her car, and drove away.

"So, both Lia and Agnes were stalking Dr. Kavanaugh, watching his apartment that night?" I asked. "Or were they stalking Emma? I'm sure it wasn't just a coincidence they were both standing out in Howard Quad."

He seemed to think about it, then took a deep breath. "I don't know about Agnes, but I think Lia wanted to blackmail Emma. Lia used to take pictures of her and Dr. Kavanaugh together. If the cops have her phone, they would see them."

I let that go for the moment. While Kavanaugh would have been susceptible to blackmail, for Emma the repercussions would only be embarrassment and loss of a mentor. The college would consider her a victim. Besides, Emma was a student. Kavanaugh was the one with money and the book.

When Kavanaugh didn't show up for class the following morning, Lia went and found Emma, who went to Katy Bosun, who went to Kavanaugh's apartment and found his body. After the police went away, taking the body with them, Lia and Josh Tupper broke into the apartment looking for the grimoire. They had done some research on the Witches' Web and hoped to sell it. They didn't find it, and within a couple of weeks, they broke up, and Lia started sleeping with Corey.

Corey told me that he knew nothing about any of it until the night of Josh's death. Josh had approached Lia at the party and tried to talk to her about the grimoire, along with a blackmail scheme. According to Corey, this scheme was something Josh dreamed up over the summer, but I got the feeling from a few things Corey said that it was something Josh and Lia had talked about before the end of the spring term. Again, when Corey spoke of blackmail, I didn't get the feeling that he really understood who was being blackmailed over what.

In any case, it led to a verbal altercation between Josh and Corey, which continued when Josh confronted the couple after they left the party. Corey knocked Josh down, Josh drew his athame, and Corey, being quite a bit larger, took it away from him.

"You didn't have to use it, you know," I pointed out.

"Yeah, that was really stupid. I was just so mad at him."

It was at that point that Corey demanded an explanation from Lia, and she told him the whole tale. Over the summer, she had discovered Trent McCarthy's offer for the grimoire, so she talked Corey into strong-arming Agnes to get it. For some reason, she had decided Agnes was the one most likely to have it, rather than Emma.

Agnes was a feisty old witch, and a lot tougher than they expected. She and Corey traded lightning bolts, and Corey got through her defenses once. Lia took the opportunity to jump on Agnes's back and stab her with her own athame. They found the grimoire in the shop's back room, then heard Kelly and me enter the shop, and ran out the back door.

"And you think that either Emma or Helen killed Lia for the book?" I asked.

"Who else?"

I didn't bother to mention George Peterson's gang, because why would they know anything about Ophelia?

"You know, even if you get off for Josh Tupper's killing by

claiming self-defense, you have no defense for Agnes Bishop's murder," I said.

"But I didn't kill her!"

I controlled the urge to roll my eyes. "Conspiracy to commit murder. Death during the commission of a felony. Those are still felonies under mundane law. And Corey, don't think you'll fare better under Council law. I know a little about their courts and processes. You don't want to go there."

"I can't believe I let her get me involved in this mess."

"So, tell me why you think Lia didn't kill herself?"

"Why would she? Guilt? Lia didn't feel guilty about Agnes. She was just afraid of being caught. Her dad is really rich, and she was very immature and self-centered. It was all a big game to her until she got arrested."

He left my place at about ten o'clock, but the ethical dilemma he'd brought with him remained. I knew that I should tell either Kagan or Barclay what Corey had told me. Or, if anyone else turned up dead, I would share the guilt.

CHAPTER 32

The following day, I dropped by Carver's office to see Katy Bosun.

"Out of curiosity, was Brett Kavanaugh dressed when you found him?" I asked.

"Yes, he was. He still had his tie on, although it was loosened, and he'd taken his jacket off and hung it up." She kind of cocked her head to look at me. "Why do you ask?"

"Well, if it was a lover, then he was probably killed before they had sex, wouldn't you agree? I can't see him getting up, putting on his shoes and tie, just to see her out to the door. And if he was driving her home, I still can't see him tying his tie."

"Hm. I see your logic, but since I never slept with him, I wouldn't know what his normal routine was."

"I'm just projecting from experiences in my younger years when occasionally I had a love life."

That afternoon, I talked Steven into driving me out to Helen's nursery in exchange for buying him dinner. I had looked the place up and found that it had gone bankrupt three years before. Helen had evidently used savings and a small loan to buy it from the bank.

When we drove up, we could see the place had a lot going for it. It sat on the west bank of the river and had about ten acres of land, with three greenhouses and a small orchard of mixed apple, pear, and peach trees. It had been a retail nursery, catering to homeowners in the area. I agreed with Helen that it should do better growing herbs, fruits, and vegetables year-round. Considering trucking distances, she could probably compete for business selling to restaurants such as the Faculty Club and Carragher's Resort in the winter.

The map I'd found showed an office building in addition to three equipment sheds, as well as a small house on the property. According to Lowell, Helen was living in the house.

The nursery as a whole looked a lot like something I could consider buying if Wicklow College continued to vie for its own show on British mystery television.

I said as much to Steven, and he replied, "Yeah, that make sense. That or I saw a bar for sale the other day."

"Is there enough LGBT business in this town to make a go of it?" I asked.

"Maybe not, but simply an inclusive, welcoming place would be nice."

"Let me guess. A place large enough to accommodate different clienteles. You know, a room for lezzies, one for gays, one for over-forty dancing, and one for nerds to play D and D."

He laughed and mentioned a place in Berkeley. "Like Lily's? I think we need to go to a city and college a little larger than Wicklow to do that sort of thing. The bar I saw was a fraction of that size."

A sign at the entrance said, 'Closed to the Public.' There was plenty of parking space in the front of the property, but following the driveway back to the house, we discovered there was barely room for a second car beside the one already parked there, and almost no space to turn around.

Helen Donnelly greeted me with a sour expression. "What do you want?"

"I'm hoping you can help me clarify a few things. Are you aware that Ophelia Harkness died yesterday?"

Her expression changed to stunned. "How?"

"She was found hanging in the greenhouse at the college. Ms. Donnelly, I'm concerned about my safety and that of others working in the garden and the greenhouse. I have a feeling this all traces back to Brett Kavanaugh's murder."

She bit her lip, gazed past me to where Steven was sitting in the car, took a deep breath, and said, "Tell your friend to come in, too. No sense sitting out there in the sun."

I waved for Steven to join me, then entered the home as Donnelly stepped aside.

She offered us seats in a small living room but no refreshments.

"There are a few students each term that harm themselves," Helen said, "but this seems awfully early, especially for a graduate student. Or do the police think it's murder?"

"I'm not sure what Sam Kagan thinks," I said, "but I think she was murdered. I keep hearing tales about something called the Gambler Grimoire. I understand there were some arguments concerning the book before Brett Kavanaugh was killed."

Helen shook her head. "That damned book. Agnes was ready to storm the battlements when she found out about it. It was like a religious crusade for her. And of course, Brett never could pass up a chance to needle her. When he found out it bothered her, he couldn't stop talking about it. I tried to mediate at first, then I tried to schedule Agnes so she wouldn't run into him. I even tried to ban him from the greenhouse, but I didn't have the authority."

"Did you ever see the book?" I asked.

"Yes, and I wasn't impressed. It looked like something a high school kid put together."

"Green with a red spine? Like a journal or a ledger book?"

"Yeah. Lined paper, and handwritten with what looked like ballpoint pen. Whether any of the spells did anything or not, I have no idea. You'd have to take it to a clairvoyant."

"A clairvoyant?"

She nodded. "Just reading a couple of the spells, you could tell they weren't designed to do anything. They were spells to enhance scrying—clairvoyance or pre-cognition. I said as much, and Brett told me I was an idiot. Hell, an idiot is someone who won't listen to a person who knows more than they do. Brett was convinced that women should have never been taught to read. I tried to get him to show it to Ruth Buckley."

The name rang a faint bell as being on the college faculty.

"Can you tell me anything about Kavanaugh's and Emma's relationship?" I asked.

Helen shrugged. "He treated her like any other pretty young thing. She was extremely respectful toward him, but I think she had a crush on him. Just the way she watched him when he wasn't looking."

"You're from Wicklow, aren't you?"

"Yes, I grew up here."

"Did you ever know a Rebecca Hall?"

Her eyes narrowed, and she stared at me like she was trying to read my mind. "Don Hall owns a hardware store downtown. He had a daughter a couple of years younger than me. Looked a lot like Emma."

"What did Emma think about that spell book?"

"She didn't get involved in the arguments, if that's what you want to know. Emma takes care of business. Not a lot of wasted motion or dreaming in that girl. Lia, on the other hand, always had her head in the clouds. I remember her asking if there really were spells that could affect the future, like a love spell or a happiness spell. I told her that planting a seed and watering it was the best spell I'd ever seen for that sort of thing."

※

On our way back to town, Steven asked, "Well, what do you think?"

"What she said about that spell book makes a lot of sense."

"Who is Rebecca Hall?"

"Emma's mother. I'm pretty sure Brett Kavanaugh was her father."

"You don't think Helen Donnelly is our killer, do you?"

"Do you?"

"Not for Ophelia. But, from what I've heard, half the town had a motive to kill Kavanaugh, simply because he was an ass, if not for any other reason."

CHAPTER 33

I thought I had it all put together, but proof was lacking. Possession of the spell book wouldn't mean much to the police, since it wasn't part of their investigation. Kelly and I had unearthed references to it, and tied it to Brett Kavanaugh's trip to London and the murder of Harold Meriweather. But even if it was found, no one had proof it was stolen.

Other than Helen Donnelly and Corey Lindsay, no one alive even admitted to having seen the book. Corey had a major reason to deny everything he'd told me, including about Ophelia's possession of the book and how she obtained it.

Five murders, and as far as I could figure out, four murderers. Maybe three, depending on whether I was willing to accept Corey's story as truthful. My theory of a daisy chain looked more accurate all the time.

And then there was the nitroglycerine hung on my front door. Ophelia had some alchemical talent, but Corey was working on a PhD in the field. Or, it could have been compounded by someone with no magical talent at all. Poisons and explosives were like that.

Over the next few days after Ophelia's death, I conducted an inventory of poisonous plants and toxins in the labs under my control. If I were the murderer, I might consider poisoning the local pain-in-the-neck when nitro didn't work. The monkshood wasn't the only deadly thing we grew in the herb garden. I made a note to myself to suggest isolating such plants from beneficial ones when we planted in the spring. And keeping track of them.

One evening after dinner, I finished washing the dishes and came out into the darkening main room of my apartment. Looking through the windows overlooking the garden, I saw the light briefly come on through the open door of my lab, and then the door shut.

The only people who had a key to that lab were Steven, Emma, and I. Everyone else had either quit, died, or both. Normally when Steve came around at odd hours, he'd stop in for a drink.

I grabbed my wand and my phone. The phone I set to record, then dropped it in the pocket of my skirt. I cast a quick spell, *"Silentium,"* before opening the door and going down the stairs to the garden.

The door to the lab was locked, but I cast a spell and heard a faint click. Easing the door open, I entered and moved through the potting area and the apothecary lab. The lights were on in the alchemy lab.

Peeking in, I saw Emma bent over a table. To one side of her, liquid was bubbling in a beaker on a hot plate. I could smell alcohol and the mixed scents of several flowers and their foliage that were lying there. On the other side of her was a slim green book with a red spine, and an older, shabbier book that looked like a grimoire.

I dropped the quiet spell. "Whipping up a love potion?" I asked.

Emma whirled around. She wore gloves, a mask, and a face

shield. Good lab practice, but usually reserved for dealing with nastier ingredients.

"That's what Lia hoped that book might contain," I continued.

The expression on Emma's face was exactly that of a kid caught with her hand in the cookie jar.

"You know, something I've been wondering is whether it would be weirder to sleep with my father or to kill him. Of course, I think my relationship with my father is probably very different than yours."

The blood drained from her face. "I-I-I never slept with him."

"But he wanted you to?"

She leaned back against the workbench. "He was often inappropriate. Yes."

"What tipped you over the edge?"

I could tell she was fishing for something to say. Emotions flitted across her face, and her mouth opened and closed a couple of times.

Then her eyes narrowed, and her posture subtly changed. "He was drunk, and made a pass at me. When I told him no, he got nasty. Said I had no talent or intelligence, and if it wasn't for him, I wouldn't have any future except to play witch in an herb shop like Agnes. I could deal with that, but then he started on my mother. He said some incredibly vile things about her, and I just snapped."

"You shouldn't have run. You should have confessed and said he attacked you and you were defending yourself. But you didn't take the book, did you?"

Her eyes darted toward it, then she shook her head. "Stupid book. No, I didn't take it. I didn't even think about it until you showed up and started asking questions."

"Why did Lia have to die?" I asked. "Was she blackmailing you?"

"Stupid bitch."

Her hand whipped up, holding her wand. *"Fulmen!"*

I held my wand before me. The lightning bolt hit it, and the crack of thunder was deafening in the small space. Smoke came from the broken end of her wand, the other half lying on the floor in front of her.

"Were you with her and Corey when they went to Agnes's shop?" I asked. "I think that was the spell that disabled Agnes. Most witches spend their whole lives and never see or engage in a mage battle. Most witches have no idea what kind of potential there is in wand magic. Of course, since you've hidden your alchemical talent, you never would have taken my course in how to craft a wand. I go into a lot of depth on the theory and materials that most people don't know about. *Praeligo!*"

With the girl bound, I pulled my phone from my pocket, ended the recording, and called Lieutenant Barclay. Maybe I should have called Kagan, but Barclay was nicer to look at.

"This is Savanna Robinson. Could you please round up Lieutenant Kagan and Chief Crumley and come to the alchemy laboratory next to the greenhouse on campus? I have an interesting tale of murder and magic you all might like to hear."

I also had a feeling that a thorough search of the greenhouse and labs could turn up some of the missing computers and books they hadn't found at Corey's.

CHAPTER 34

A group of people who had become my friends in Wicklow sat around a table in a corner of the Faculty Club. I was doing my best to ignore the shots someone had bought for me, and was sticking to wine. I realized I needed to slow down on the wine, too.

"Let me get this straight," David Hamilton said, "this girl was Brett's daughter? Did he know this when she came to school here?"

"I'm pretty sure he did. I know that he paid child support for another of his daughters who grew up here in town. My understanding is that Emma had spent a few summers here with her grandparents when she was growing up. Whether she ever saw him then, I don't know. Her grandfather wasn't one of Brett's biggest fans."

"I would guess not," Kelly said. "So, Emma beat his head in because he was being a lech and a jerk, then she ran, but she was seen?"

"Yes, that stupid book. Ophelia and Agnes were watching. I don't think they were together, and I don't know if they were watching Brett or Emma. Both wanted the book. Probably both had an interest in blackmailing him. When he turned up dead, Ophelia, at least, switched her blackmail to Emma. It was all a game to her."

"And how does Joshua Tupper fit into all this?" Hamilton asked.

"This happened before Ophelia broke up with him. He was angry with her, jealous of Corey, and had fantasies of selling the book for a lot of money. In his mind, she cheated him out of his half of the book proceeds."

"Speaking of which, what is going on with the book?" Steven asked. When I had recovered it and given it to Kelly, we discovered the title of it on an inside page was 'Spells to Foretell the Future.' The cover itself was blank. Analysis of the physical book placed its manufacture as sometime in the 1950s.

"Ruth Buckley, who is a professor of divination, took a look at it," Kelly said. "Evidently the spells it contains are for divination, scrying, and pre-cognition. Basically, if you cast them while asking a question as to whether something might happen, most of the spells will return a yes or no answer."

"That could still be useful," Lowell said.

Kelly cocked her head. "Yes, but you're not going to spend five or ten minutes casting a spell to find out if the next cast of the dice will be a seven or not. And it doesn't do you much good to know if a stock will go up tomorrow, since it wouldn't tell you if it goes up three cents or three dollars, now would it?"

"And it wouldn't tell you what it would do the following day," David said. "There are a lot of magic spells that are basically useless."

"Exactly. Ruth said that one of the spells might tell you if the plane you are taking tomorrow will crash," I said. "Considering that the grand majority of planes don't crash, you could cast the spell several thousand times, and unless a plane crashed, you still wouldn't know if the spell really worked or not."

"So, Agnes ended up with the book," David said. "And everyone sort of forgot about it until you showed up."

"I guess. Ophelia did a lot of research over the summer, discovered Trent McCarthy's offer, and decided she could use a little extra cash. I still haven't figured out if Emma went to Agnes along with Ophelia and Corey, but at least the latter two tried to strong-arm her. It was about that time that Emma started to worry about Ophelia. She has smartly clammed up and is hiding behind her lawyer."

"Has anyone contacted Trent McCarthy about the book?" Steven asked.

"Edmund—Dr. Phillips—has," Kelly said. "Sent him a few pictures of it. Not to sell it, just as a professional courtesy so he would know it exists and that we have it. McCarthy said he had seen something similar but wouldn't pay ten cents for it."

"Any idea what the worth of that other book is?" I asked.

"The *Maleficium*? Priceless, and not for sale. We notified the Council, and as the Wicklow Museum is a certified repository, we've locked it away in the deepest depths of our archives. Available to Council-certified researchers for limited study."

"Where could he have acquired such a thing?" I asked.

"Somewhere in his travels," Lowell said. "Definitely not from Harold or me. If I had to guess, somewhere in Eastern Europe or the Middle East or India. There are dealers who are not registered with the Council. I'm convinced he got it from someone who really didn't know what it was. Very possibly a non-witch. Brett didn't have the money to afford it otherwise."

"Do you suppose there really is a Gambler Grimoire?" I asked.

"Possibly," Kelly said.

"How about a Wandsmith Grimoire?" David asked. "Some of the more esoteric branches of magic might never have been codified."

"That wand of yours is very unusual," Lowell said.

"And expensive, I'll bet," Kelly chimed in. The check for sixty thousand dollars from Kelly's mom had come in—proceeds for five wands Harold Merriweather had sold for me.

I shrugged. "The materials alone are too expensive for me to duplicate it. I traded a custom wand to a gemstone broker in Antwerp for the ruby at the tip. The inner bark of oak, rowan, willow, and yew are braided together and left flexible, fixed inside to the stiff handle of applewood by a cabochon of amber with an included wasp, set using owl talons. The moonstone on the pommel is set with talons from a kestrel. The entire wand is sheathed in kelpie hide bound with silver. Each part of the manufacture is carried out during a different phase of the moon, and the final binding and blessing was done on a full moon during Summer Solstice. Such timing requires some planning."

"Kelpie hide?" Lowell asked, laughing. "And where would you be getting that?"

"I was in a pub in a town on the coast near Edinburgh when a young man picked me up and took me for a ride. I knew something was wrong when he leaped off a cliff into the sea. It was touch and go for a while, but I managed to drown him and drag the body to shore. It was a full moon, and it took me until dawn to skin him."

"You're pulling my leg," Steven said.

"You drowned a kelpie?" David appeared quite skeptical.

Lowell punched him in the shoulder. "There's no such thing as a kelpie."

"Of course. If he had drowned me, I wouldn't be here to tell the story, now, would I?"

Some of my friends were staring at me with open skepticism. Kelly was laughing so hard tears were running down her cheeks.

"A ride. I'll bet. Goddess, I need to go on holiday with you. And how much for a common, run-of-the-mill Savanna

Robinson custom wand?" Kelly asked when she finished laughing. "I'll forego the kelpie hide."

"Ten to twenty-five thousand retail. I'd give you a twenty-five percent discount because you're a friend. Considering my time, I really don't make much from a wand." I looked to Lowell. "Now that Harold's out of business, are you interested in peddling a wand for me now and then?"

"I would be happy to let people know if one were available." He gave me a faint smile and a wink. "Of course, any good word put in with your father would be appreciated. I've never known a daughter of a councilman before."

If you enjoyed **The Gambler Grimoire**, I hope you will take a few moments to leave a brief review on the site where you purchased your copy. It helps to share your experience with other readers. Potential readers depend on comments from people like you to help guide their purchasing decisions. Thank you for your time!

Get updates on new book releases, promotions, contests and giveaways!
Sign up for my newsletter.

BOOKS BY BR KINGSOLVER

Wicklow College of Arcane Arts

The Gambler Grimoire

The Revenge Game

The Rift Chronicles

Magitek

War Song

Soul Harvest

Rosie O'Grady's Paranormal Bar and Grill

Shadow Hunter

Night Stalker

Dark Dancer

Well of Magic

Knights Magica

The Dark Streets Series

Gods and Demons

Dragon's Egg

Witches' Brew

The Chameleon Assassin Series

Chameleon Assassin

Chameleon Uncovered

Chameleon's Challenge

Chameleon's Death Dance

Diamonds and Blood

The Telepathic Clans Saga
The Succubus Gift
Succubus Unleashed
Broken Dolls
Succubus Rising
Succubus Ascendant

Other books
I'll Sing for my Dinner
Trust

Short Stories in Anthologies
Here, Kitty Kitty
Bellator

~~~

Printed in Great Britain
by Amazon